DEEP INTO THE GAME

GAMELAND

episode one

GOT A TASTE FOR THE UNDEAD?

CHECK OUT THESE THRILLERS
ALSO FROM THE MIND OF SAUL TANPEPPER

GAMELAND series

Golgotha (prequel to GAMELAND)

Episode Two: *Failsafe*

Episode Three: *Deadman's Switch*

Episode Four: *Sunder the Hollow Ones*

Episode Five: *Prometheus Wept*

Episode Six: *Kingdom of Players*

Episode Seven: *Tag, You're Dead*

Episode Eight: *Jacker's Code*

Collections

Undead and Other Horrors

Insomnia

Short Stories

The Headhunter

A Thing for Zombies

Outsourced

Raise the Dead

Occupied

Flawless: a Claire Fontaine novella

(turn to the back of this book for availability)

GAMELAND

episode one

DEEP INTO THE GAME

by

Saul Tanpepper

BRINESTONE PRESS
San Martin, CA

GAMELAND
Episode One: *Deep Into the Game*

‡ ‡ ‡

Copyright © 2012 by Saul Tanpepper
Cover and interior art by Ken J. Howe
Design by Brinestone Press Copyright © 2012

Type set in Eurostile 11 point

All rights reserved.

Brinestone Press
http://www.brinestonepress.com

PUBLISHER'S NOTE:

This book is a work of fiction. Names, characters, places, and incidents either are the product of the author's imagination or are used fictitiously, and any resemblance to actual persons, living or dead, business establishments, events, or locales is entirely coincidental.

No portion of this book may be reproduced by any means, mechanical, electronic, or otherwise, without first obtaining the permission of the copyright holder.

For more information, contact Brinestone Press or the author at:

editor@brinestonepress.com

authorsaultanpepper@gmail.com

ISBN-13: 978-1-479-17755-4 (soft cover)
ISBN-10: 1-479-17755-5 (soft cover)

10 9 8 7 6 5 4 3 2
130220

Contents

Welcome to GAMELAND	vii
Prologue	1
Part One: The Plan. Or Rather the Pathetic Lack of One	
Chapter One	10
Chapter Two	17
Chapter Three	21
Chapter Four	26
Chapter Five	34
Chapter Six	36
Chapter Seven	38
Chapter Eight	42
Chapter Nine	47
Chapter Ten	53
Chapter Eleven	55
Chapter Twelve	61
Part Two: Breaking In	
Chapter Thirteen	64
Chapter Fourteen	71
Chapter Fifteen	75
Chapter Sixteen	79
Chapter Seventeen	83
Chapter Eighteen	86
Chapter Nineteen	90
Chapter Twenty	96
Chapter Twenty One	102
Chapter Twenty Two	107
Chapter Twenty Three	111
ACKNOWLEDGEMENTS	118
ABOUT THE AUTHOR	119
CURRENT TITLES IN THE GAMELAND SERIES	120
WHERE TO FIND MY BOOKS	122

Welcome to GAMELAND

Dear Friend, a quick word about GAMELAND:

First off, a heartfelt thanks for taking that leap of faith when you purchased this book. If this is your first introduction to my work, I hope you'll find the experience worthy of your continued patronage. If you've enjoyed my other titles, I'm thrilled you're back. It's my fervent wish that this new effort exceeds your every expectation.

GAMELAND was the brainchild of discussions between myself and my publisher, Brinestone Press, back in 2011. Together, we fleshed out an overarching storyline to be told over the course of several books. Each action-packed 'episode' features a group of recurring characters, has its own theme, and works out its own particular issues. Structurally, the series is modeled after popular television shows (think *Fringe, Bones, The Walking Dead*), with each episode roughly the equivalent of a two-hour commercial-free program. At the story level, however, GAMELAND is wholly unique, a mix of cyberpunk, horror, suspense and mystery.

What you've purchased is the first of these eight episodes. In a sense, this is the series 'pilot' and so it introduces you to the main characters, their foibles and strengths, their world and the issues confronting them. The larger story issues will mature over the course of the series. It is my hope that you'll enjoy this work, both as a separate and independent experience, but also recognizing that it exists in a much larger framework.

If you would like news about the GAMELAND series, just shoot me an email to **authorsaultanpepper@gmail.com** and ask me to add you to the GAMELAND mailing list, or subscribe to the *Tanpepper Tidings* newsletter at:
https://tinyletter.com/SWTanpepper.

I am also on Facebook, where I am hosting a growing community of fans. I'd love to see you there. I encourage you to visit and "Like" the GAMELAND fan page where I post updates, discussions and other news about the series. For links, turn to pages 117-118.

Lastly, I value your opinion and so encourage you to offer your thoughts on this work, either positive or negative, whether you choose to do so publicly or privately. I want to know what you think and promise you that I will always give your feedback serious consideration. Note that I do not engage reviewers or their posted comments in public. I want my readers to feel comfortable expressing their honest and thoughtful opinions without fear of being stalked by me.

Now, sit back and enjoy *The Game*. I hope to see you back for the next installment of GAMELAND.

Saul
San Francisco, CA
Feb 20, 2013

GAMELAND

DEEP INTO THE GAME

Prologue

Fifteen years after Golgotha

It wasn't Reggie's idea to break into Gameland, not initially, though of course he took all the credit. He liked being the go-to guy whenever it was something the five of us could all get behind. He was funny that way — a big brute of a kid with all kinds of brains and good looks and a huge gaping insecurity complex that needed constant attention. But whenever something turned out to be not so good after all, he was usually the first to distance himself from it, claiming he always knew it was a bad idea, right from the beginning. That's just the way he was.

He had a way of picking the bad ideas, which is why we should've just said no.

We were in Micah's basement. He and Kelly were team-playing *Zpocalypto*, which is supposed to be something like *The Game*. Except it turned out to be nothing like it at all. First of all, it was nowhere near as real. There's no VR and the action's totally lame. Plus, the holographics are just so-so. You don't get a good feel for what it's like to be in the actual Gameland, fighting actual zombies, trying not to get eaten. Now I know.

I also know this: Not even those lucky rich pricks have any idea what it's like, the ones who are connected enough to pay for a state-of-the-art cybernetic setup and a Player, *plus* weasel the necessary invite into *The Game*. Arc Entertainment didn't just let anyone play. They only wanted the best.

Like us.

Reg and I were bookending the couch. Ashley was sprawled out between us, her feet on his lap and her head on mine. She was drinking a Red Bull through a straw, the can wedged between two cushions to keep it upright. Reg had chugged his and had tossed the empty at the old milk crate in the corner. He missed, of course, and blamed it on the lighting, which admittedly was piss-poor. Micah's HG setup was old and glitchy, so he had to keep the lights dimmed.

Reg was antsy. He was always antsy, but probably more so then because of the caffeine. He kept asking us if we were finished with our drinks. I'm sure he thought the first miss was just a fluke and wanted to redeem himself. That's how self-deluded he could be. But I'd barely even touched my RB. I like the taste of it, but the stuff gives me a headache if I drink it too quickly. And Ash was purposefully nursing hers just to be a pissant.

I was messing with her coppery hair, twining it between my fingers, trying to straighten the curls and watching them spring back. For some reason it struck me as comical and I kept giggling, even though I wasn't even the slightest bit drunk or stoned. Not like Micah. He was the druggie in the group.

The rest of us got our highs playing games or hacking them. That was our escape from the misfortune of being born into families that couldn't afford to buy a decent entertainment system. My family was once so lucky, but after my dad died and Grandpa was fired from his prestigious command post in the Marines, that all went away. Of course, that all happened fifteen or so years ago, so as far as I could remember we'd always been as poor and out-of-the-loop as anyone else in that room.

I caught Reg glancing over at us — probably envisioning me and Ash acting out one of his perverted girl-on-girl fantasies. I obliged him. Sort of. I reached over and pinched Ash's nose until she slapped my hand away with an inviting shriek. The movement caused her to dig her heels into Reggie's crotch, which was precisely what I was going for. I saw him jerk in pain. He tried to hide it, but I saw.

"What's so funny, Jess?" Ash asked me, gazing up at me with those brilliant green eyes of hers. They were so innocent looking, but I'd always known how manipulative they could be.

"Nothing," I answered. Then I coughed, trying to hide another snort of laughter.

Reggie groaned out loud. Then, trying to hide his discomfort, he started complaining about how bored he was: "This scene blows, guys," he whined. "You know what we should do? We should break into Gameland."

"We already tried, Reg. Remember?" Kelly replied. He was referring to Ash's and Micah's attempt to hack *The Game* a couple weeks earlier. But I sensed that Reggie was talking about something else altogether, something a hell of lot more illegal and a shit-load more dangerous.

I watched as Kel's and Micah's zombie hunters searched through a dark warehouse looking for food. I'd never played this level before, but I could guess what was going to happen. There were certain patterns to how *Zpocalypto* was constructed. Once you recognized them, it was a lot easier to survive and advance to the next level. If my guess was correct, they were about to be jumped by a bunch of the Undead at any moment.

"Not *The Game*, dweeb," Reggie barked. "I'm talking about breaking into Long Island itself. We should actually physically *go* there ourselves."

Kelly didn't look up. "Yeah, man. We'll just hop onto the next transit over there right now." He exhaled with disgust when a zombie slipped out of a shipping crate and chomped down on his ankle, immediately crippling him. If he didn't make it back to his antivenin kit within the next few minutes, his character would be dead and return to undo everything he'd accomplished to get this far.

The "antivenin kit" was one of those things that irritated me the most about *Zpocalypto*. First of all, the bite causes an infection; it's not a poison, like a snake bite. They should've called it an anti-infective. Secondly, in real life, if you're bitten, there is no cure. What's the saying? Once bitten, twice dead? That professor who tried fifteen years ago proved that. The one who everyone says killed my father.

"I'm not talking right this minute, brah," Reggie answered.

"I'm up for it!" Micah said, as he lopped the virtual head off a virtual zombie with a virtual light saber, something the game was obviously not programmed to provide.

Ash raised her head and looked at me in disgust after seeing this. I just shrugged. It didn't surprise me anymore. Micah was always reprogramming the game in his favor.

"But we should try soon," he added, throwing the severed head into his virtual backpack. "Like, this weekend."

"Where'd you get the light saber?" Kelly asked. He sounded jealous.

Micah smiled his shit-eating grin. "I did a little creative recoding yesterday."

"Cheater."

"Well . . . yeah."

"Why this weekend?" I asked, only because I was curious to see how far the boys were willing to take this conversation. Theorizing something as blatantly illegal as breaking into LI was much more entertaining than watching the boys play a game they'd hacked. It was also more entertaining than seeing how springy Ashley's hair could be. Or causing Reggie bodily harm and insult.

"Because in two and a half short weeks, our lives are totally going to be over, girl. That's why."

Micah was referring to the start of our senior year in high school. Well, Ash would technically be only a junior, but she had enough credits to graduate with the rest of us, and probably would.

Just three more weekends before our last year of incarceration. Nineteen more days of parole before we were all swallowed up in that mess of a penal system that masqueraded as a social welfare program. It was ostensibly there to prepare us for the harsh realities of an even harsher world, but it failed to do so on so many levels that it was almost ridiculous.

As far as the majority of kids my age were concerned, school was just another relic of the past. How was studying mid-sixteenth century literature supposed to help us deal with rising sea levels in the mid-twenty first century? How was knowing the sum of the angles of a triangle going to help us in the event of another outbreak? If it wasn't for the fact that getting caught skipping school was pretty much a death sentence, signing years of our afterlife away into conscription, we wouldn't even bother going.

I exhaled, trying to quell the sense of panic and anticipation rising up inside of me. I didn't like to be reminded of time slipping away, of what awaited us on the other side of August. I reminded myself that I had to suffer only one more year of that institutionalized prison, then I'd be free to do whatever I wanted to do. We all would.

Most of us were planning on skipping college and going straight into one of those high-paying jobs as a coder with ArcWare. Kelly was the only one of us giving college any serious thought. He was always the one who had to be different from the rest of us. That's what first attracted me to him, his long view, and it's what I so dearly loved about him.

Out of all the guys I'd ever known, he was the kindest, the most caring. Anyone who knew the Corben family — who knew Kyle, Kelly's little brother — could see that.

On the outside, Kelly wasn't much to talk about: brown hair and eyes, an average build, average looks. A girlfriend probably shouldn't say this about her boyfriend, but he was ... forgettable. Nevertheless, he more than made up for it with his earnestness. I'd rather be with a guy who was honest with me than one who was easy on the eyes.

Lately, though, he'd been acting all strange. He was moody, inattentive, distracted. Just once in a while I wished he'd lighten up and relax.

"Wait," he said. "You're not serious, are you?" He jerked his body to the left, then twisted it as he tried to get his player to respond faster in the game, but the cheap sensors were low-res and iffy and it made his hunter look more like one of the hunted, all lurchy and uncoordinated. "You mean, like, actually *break into* Long Island?"

"Dead serious, brah," Reggie replied. He laughed, probably realizing he'd inadvertently made a funny.

Reggie was Kel's opposite. In fact, he was pretty much the opposite of any of us. "Big, bald and brash," Micah always said about him, a stark contrast to his own blond, blue-eyed, befreckled boyish good looks and charm. "A brute with a heart the size of Texas."

And Micah would certainly know about Texas. He was once a Republic good old boy before his parents defected to Connecticut. He always had a smile on his face and a reputation for never hurting a soul. A *living* soul, that is. When it came to zombies, on the other hand, he was a stone-cold killer. The Undead rarely stood a chance against him. He was the best game player I'd ever seen. Probably the best hacker, too.

Kelly wasn't nearly as good as Micah in the gaming department — or me, for that matter — but still a hell of a lot better than most. Better than Reggie, anyway. And while he could hack, he didn't like doing it. He was too uptight for any of that action, though not enough to not hang out with us.

Yet, as different as the three boys were, they were all brilliant, and they all shared the same passion for gaming. We all did, which is what brought us together in the first place. It's what kept us together despite the immense differences in our personalities.

"Why would we even want to go to the Wastes?" Kelly asked without looking away. The Wastes were the places that had been decimated over the past thirty years by rising sea levels. Pretty much every coastal city had such areas, variably referred to as the Wastes or Wastelands. They were urban ghost towns, and LI was just one of many. Perfect breeding grounds for outbreaks.

Reggie shrugged. "Uh, no reason, brah, other than to see if we actually can. To say that we did."

"Sure, why not," Ashley chimed in. "I'll try anything once. We haven't done a damn thing exciting all summer and it's almost over!"

I wanted to pinch her nose again just for reminding me of that.

The more I thought about it, the more I realized how breaking into Long Island — even just *planning* something like it — would liven things up, take our minds off of school and the inevitable dreariness of those long winter days ahead, hunched over a desk in sub-zero classrooms, suffering the slings and arrows of outrageous Shakespeare-inflicted misfortune.

This time Ashley didn't ask why I was giggling.

"Doing something just so you can brag about it isn't a reason," Kelly argued.

"Oh, don't be such a weenie," Reggie retorted. It was his typical comeback whenever any of us disagreed with something he said. We usually let him get away with it because he was so damn big. That, and he actually relished a good argument.

But Kelly wasn't giving in so easily. They got into a heated discussion, mostly focusing on the actual logistics of breaking into what had once been a militarized zone and was now blockaded by physical and electromagnetic barriers.

I was listening with interest, but Ash got bored and made me go upstairs with her. She needed to use the bathroom and the one down in the basement was nasty. But she never liked wandering around Micah's upstairs all alone. She said it felt spooky, like his parents were ghosts watching over her.

When we came back down, it appeared that the argument was over. Micah and Kelly were back to playing *Zpocalypto* and Reggie was asleep on the couch, snoring loudly. He had a smile on his face.

Ashley kicked him. "Hey, perv! Make some room," she said. "Quit hogging the couch."

Reggie opened one eye and his smile widened, but he didn't move. "Where'd you guys go?"

"Upstairs to have hot lesbian sex in Micah's room."

"That was quick."

"Yeah, well, Jessie's super easy to bring to climax."

"Ashley!"

I could feel my face burning. I may have lost my virginity at fifteen, but I was still a bit of a prude about it, especially around her. It was like I needed to balance out her own over-the-top sexuality.

Ash didn't care what people thought. She always just said whatever was on her mind. In fact, I'm sure she said things just to try and elicit a reaction.

I looked over at Kelly, but he hadn't even heard what she'd said. He was too absorbed in the game.

Reggie snorted. He gave Ash a good, long, appraising look, beginning with the thumbs she'd hooked onto the waistband of her jeans, pausing at the low neckline of her more-than-ample breasts, then finally reaching her eyes. Not once did she flinch. If anything, the look on her face grew even more defiant.

"Sorry I missed it," he said.

She glanced pointedly at the bulge in his jeans and smiled. "I'm sure it was just as exciting as you imagined it."

Reggie laughed and pulled up his legs, then swung them over the front of the couch. Ash plunked down next to him with a heavy exhale. He swung his arm over her shoulders, letting his fingers dangle a hair's width away from the top of her breast. Though the two weren't technically together, everyone knew they were doing it. At least whenever there wasn't anything better going on. Or any*one*.

I glanced past my boyfriend to the flickering HG image in front of him. He was back to level eleven — his nemesis. If I were a betting girl, I'd wager he was on his last life and was about to be attacked. Again.

Poor Kelly. As good as he was, he just couldn't seem to make it past this level no matter how many times he tried. But I didn't feel much pity for him at the moment. Sometimes, like right now when he wasn't paying any attention to me, his obsession with the game kind of pissed me off.

"So . . . what'd you guys decide?" Ashley asked. "About Gameland."

I looked over. Reggie's thumb was now resting on the exposed skin of her breast. He was slowly brushing it back and forth. I felt a tingle pass through my own body, then a twinge of jealousy. Reggie was a code geek, just like the rest of us, but at least he had broader interests outside of the games.

Kelly could learn a thing or two from his example.

"Well, actually, it wouldn't technically be Gameland," he told Ash. "We'd just be breaking into one of the Forbidden Zones on LI — an *outer* zone. I think the Gameland arena is more toward the center of the island — that's what Micah thinks, anyway — and it's probably pretty heavily barricaded to keep the Players from getting out."

He was talking about the implanted zombies that were recruited into *The Game*. They called them Players.

"There's still the Infected Undead on the rest of the island," I pointed out.

Reggie chuffed. "Yeah, like there'd be any IUs left after thirteen years. They're all dead by now." He waggled his fingers spookily at me and said, "No brains to feed on."

"You don't know that."

He shook his head. "You're beginning to sound just like your boyfriend. He says it's not doable."

"I didn't say that."

Reggie smiled. He was egging me on, and I'd fallen for it. I should've known. Whatever Kelly said, Reg always tried to say the opposite. And now that Kelly was saying it was impossible to break into LI, it just made Reg even more determined to say it wasn't.

Kelly paused his game so he could tick reasons off on his fingers: "Fifty foot wall around the entire island, electrified razor wire, all the bridges demoed, no-fly zones, biometric mines in the East River, electromagnetic barrier—"

"EM, brah? Really? Chillax. I'm not talking about *hacking* in, I'm talking about breaking in. Remember? The EM's nothing to worry about."

"It could fry your implant," I said.

"Implant, shmimplant."

"There's no way," Kelly insisted. "I'm telling you, it's impossible."

"Maybe there is a way," Micah said, still playing. He was one of those freaky types who could give a hundred percent of his attention to something like *Zpocalypto* or *Warlock Four* and yet still be fully involved in a conversation, even while being stoned off his gourd. I could never understand how he did it. The guy was more than just scary smart. It was like he could partition his brain into distinct segments — one for gaming, one for being wasted, one for everything else — yet still use them all at full capacity. He was like a computer. "I'll give it some thought."

"I know!" Ashley exclaimed. "We'll just sprinkle a little fairy dust on our bodies and fly ourselves in."

"I'll sprinkle fairy dust over your body if you do mine," Reggie said.

I snorted.

He looked over at me. "Every time someone disses a fairy, another zombie gets its wings."

I rolled my eyes, but I was laughing.

"That's just... stupid!" Kelly snapped. "Besides, you have to get through Manhattan's restricted zones first. That can be a hassle."

"That's true," I said. I'd gone there on occasion with my brother; he had a special pass. I remembered all the checkpoints and the guards questioning us.

Kelly smiled and nodded at me, thinking I was actually taking his side in the argument. "It's crazy talk."

I went over and plopped down on his lap and planted a kiss on his lips. It wasn't one of our usual hot-n-heavy lip-bruising kisses — I didn't want to start anything — but I hoped it was enough that he'd not take what I was about to say the wrong way.

"If Reggie says he can come up with a plan, then . . . . Well, I'm in, too."

Kelly leaned away from me like I was contagious.

Reggie gave a howl of triumph. "See? Didn't I tell you it was a good idea?"

† † †

That was weeks ago now. How many exactly, I don't know. I've lost count of the days.

Reggie is leaning on me, pushing all of his weight onto the bandage pressed at my side as if he's afraid my guts are going to come spilling out at any moment. Now he doesn't look so sure of himself.

"I knew this was bad," he growls. "Right from the start I knew we shouldn't have come here. That's what I tried to tell you guys."

I look up at Kelly standing outside the glass door looking in — what's left of him, anyway — and I see now that he was right. He was right all along. I just wish he'd tried harder to stop us.

I don't blame either of them, though. I don't blame anyone. Not myself, not even the asshole who first planted the idea in Reggie's brain. We all had our own private reason for coming. That's what really drove us to do it. But would we have come if we knew then what we know now? Would we still have agreed to try?

I don't know. Maybe not.

Then again, maybe.

As I lie here dying, lost somewhere in the Wastes with zombies closing in, wanting nothing more than to feed on those of us still alive, the truth finally hits home: it never really mattered what we wanted or didn't want. Arc Entertainment had this all planned from the very beginning. They wanted us in *The Game*. That's why it was so easy for us to break in.

And why getting out has been such a killer.

I slowly reach behind my back, to the cold metal of the gun tucked into my waistband. I've got one bullet left. Just one. I know it sounds cliché, but I've been saving it for just such a moment.

My fingers wrap around the grip; they find the safety and flick it off. They touch the curve of the trigger, test its resistance. Reggie sees the wince on my face as I pull it free, but he thinks it's just the infection taking hold. He doesn't yet see the gun. All he knows is that the disease is spreading inside of me. He knows the agony I'll soon be going through. He knows the monster I'm about to become.

I cough. "Got any antivenin?" I ask, trying for humor.

He smiles a wistful smile.

I draw the gun out and hold it up. They all see it at the same moment, though it doesn't register with any of them right away what I'm going to do with it. Then, all at once, they know, and they start yelling for me not to do it.

But I don't hear them. All I can hear as I aim and pull the trigger is Kelly — my poor, dear, lost Kelly — whispering inside my head how much he loves me.

I guess he was a better player than I realized.

Part One

The Plan. Or Rather the Pathetic Lack of One

Chapter One

Two days before breaking in.

Thursday mornings during the summer are set aside for free sparring at the dojang. I've been studying hapkido since I was nine and recently passed my 1st gup black belt. What prompted my older brother Eric to push me into martial arts was the second outbreak, the one that happened down in DC. He thought a little self-defense training might come in handy.

The problem with that kind of thinking is that nobody believes a bunch of fancy kicks and holds is any kind of defense against the Infected Undead. And especially not against those with implants. I'd seen the Omegaman propaganda videos in school and knew the damage they could do to a person when fully under the control of a functioning L.I.N.C. implant. But since the government only just started making them mandatory about ten years ago, there are still tons of people who don't have one yet, just waiting to become an IU in the event of another outbreak.

So, yeah, while guns have their shortcomings, I'd rather have one than not.

Despite knowing all that, I decided to stick with the training anyway. I had other reasons for doing so. For one thing, it helped me manage my anger. For another, it kept the bullies who knew my family's history from kicking my ass.

The first outbreak took place in New York, on Long Island, but I don't really remember it. I was maybe four at the time. Eric says it was terrible. The one in Washington wasn't as bad. The military had some experience dealing with thousands of IUs swarming through cities by then. It's probably why DC was never abandoned like LI was. That, and because the island was already pretty trashed from the flooding earlier in the century. As it turns out, it looks like that flooding may provide us the means to break in.

Ashley pinged me last night during dinner to tell me that Micah and Reg had been working on figuring out a way to access LI without passing through the EM barrier. "They think they've come up with a working plan!" She'd sounded excited, breathless. Despite my own doubts, I couldn't resist getting excited, too.

"And?" I'd asked, trying not to sound impatient. "What is it?"

Eric threw me a dirty look over the table. I ignored him. He's always tried to take care of me like a parent, given how there was a huge gaping vacuum in our lives in that regard, but he's barely able to care of himself, much less me. Even his department-mandated shrink tells him that.

"So," Ash said, "you know how everyone knows about the wall and no-fly zone, right?"

I grunted. It was all common knowledge. Plus the bridges, which were bombed out years back. I thought about mentioning how the East River was heavily mined, but I knew it would just make me sound like Kelly. And besides, it was a moot point anyway. None of us had a boat, or even access to one, so sailing across the river was out of the question. Mostly, though, I just kept quiet because Eric and Grandpa were sitting right there, trying not to look like they were listening, but not fooling anyone.

I turned my back and held my Link tight against me ear.

"Jessie?" Grandpa said. "Dinnertime is family time, young lady. Disconnect, please."

"I'm sorry. This is important. I really have to take this." I got up and slipped out of the kitchen.

"Jessie!" Eric called. "It can't be that important."

I heard Grandpa tell him to control himself, which, of course, led to another argument between them. I never understood the animosity the two shared for each other — frankly, I couldn't care less — except for being aware that it had something to do with my father dying when I was two. Eric had been fourteen at the time, so he still has memories of Dad and all that happened after his death. It really messed him up.

Pretty much everything in my family traces back to that singular event, like it was some kind of Big Bang event or something: my mom's nervous breakdown, Eric's pacifist days followed by his stint in the Marines followed by his creepy obsession with the Undead, Grandpa's scandal and then coming to live with us. I'd never known my father — except by reputation — so I never really felt much interest in learning about him and the circumstances surrounding how he'd died. At least he had the good sense to be murdered before the Life Service law was passed. Not that the government would've had much to work with in his case; from what little I knew, most of his brain had never been found. And without a brain, there's no chance of reanimation.

I hurried down the hall and slipped into the bathroom and closed the door. Ash was saying something about tunnels. I barely caught the tail-end of it.

"What tunnels?"

"Micah thinks he can get his hands on some of the old subway maps and traffic tunnels connecting Manhattan and Long Island."

"From where? How?"

As far as I knew, all of the old plans and schematics had been collected and destroyed after LI was militarized and the wall was built. It was against the law to possess anything related to them. I think it was more an act of denial by the government than one of defiance or security. They probably would've gone in and nuked the place if they could've gotten away with it, if the radioactive ash cloud didn't take out a million more people, making them ripe for reanimation.

"Micah says nothing's ever totally lost, not once it's been in the Stream. There are off-line archives. Someone somewhere is bound to have their own file. Or hardcopy. It just takes a little time to find someone willing to sell the information."

"Where are we going to get the money? And isn't that illegal?"

"Shh!"

I thought about this for a moment, then shook my head. "I'm sure the tunnels are all bombed out or filled in. It wouldn't make sense to just leave them open for zombies to walk through to Manhattan. Otherwise, we'd be seeing a lot more of them, right?"

"First of all, Jess, I think Reggie's right: there aren't any more IUs alive on the island. Second of all, the tunnels were flooded before the first outbreak. Remember? And everyone knows zombies can't swim."

I snorted. Duh. She was right, of course. After that massive ice shelf broke off of Antarctica nearly thirty years ago and caused the sea levels to surge higher by thirty feet, most of the underground transportation networks in coastal cities had to be abandoned. I guess I hadn't really paid very close attention in history class that day.

"What about the tunnel openings?" I asked. "They'd still be above water, wouldn't they? Surely when the wall was built, they would've closed them—"

"The wall was built ten years ago."

"Okay . . . ."

"Don't you see? *After* the second flood. The openings would've been totally underwater already. Micah thinks they wouldn't have bothered blockading them since they'd be covered by a good twenty feet of Atlantic Ocean. Out of sight, out of mind, as he says. What's even better, if they're still open, then we can totally bypass the EM barrier by going *under* it! No walls, no razor wire. It's perfect!"

I shook my head. "I don't know . . . . It sounds like wishful thinking to me. And anyway, the last time I checked, I didn't have gills. And neither do you or anyone else I know."

"Reggie's looking into that."

"Reggie? What's he going to do, rent us a sub or something?"

Ash laughed. "No, silly. The sensors would totally detect something that big, even going through the tunnels. He's thinking a bit . . . smaller, something more personalized."

I asked her what, but she wouldn't elucidate.

It seemed plausible, and yet I still had my doubts. It was almost too easy. If one of us could come up with a solution like that so quickly, then surely others would have already done so as well.

But then I realized why that wasn't likely. Most normal people avoided lower Manhattan like the plague. And even if you had to go there, the closer you got to LI, the harder it was with all the checkpoints you had to cross. Besides, who in their right mind would seriously think about breaking in? No one was crazy enough to actually want to. They called them Forbidden Zones for a reason, not Disney-Arc Land.

I mentioned this to Ash.

"That's where your brother might come in handy," she said.

I knew exactly what she was talking about: Eric's permit. But before I could argue about it there was a knock on the door. "Jess?" It was my grandfather. "Come out here, young lady, and finish your dinner."

"Just a sec," I yelled. "Ash, I got to go." I lowered my voice to a whisper and added, "You know how the Colonel gets."

"Yes sir!" Ash said, giggling. "I'll get right on spit shining my dinner plate with my tongue, sir!"

I laughed and told her I'd think about it, then we disconnected.

When I stepped out of the bathroom, Grandpa was just making his way back down the hallway. He turned and gave me a stern look and told me to go finish my dinner. I was so excited that I almost shouted, "Yes sir!" just like Ash had done.

I love Grandpa, but there's one thing you never do and that's antagonize him. You take your life into your own hands. The only reason Eric gets away with it is because he's just as bullheaded as Grandpa is.

And, honestly? I think Grandpa's a little afraid of him.

† † †

It's a beautiful August morning by the time I leave the house for the dojang. The sun's still low on the horizon and it's not too muggy out. Not yet, anyway. The cicadas are singing in the trees. I almost feel like skipping all the way there.

The studio opens at seven, though I usually don't show up until around eight thirty. This morning, however, I'd been too wound up to sleep in, as thoughts about actually getting to see a part of the Forbidden Zones suddenly take on a more realistic feel to them. I'm earlier than usual — only the third person to arrive — so I'm left without a sparring partner and will have to wait.

Kwanjangnim Rupert is with some guy I don't know, a green belt. They're walking off the mat as I sign in, looking like they've just finished up their first sparring exercises. They go straight into their meditations. I can hear the master talking about *Yu*, the water principle: "The stream flows around and surrounds its obstacles," he quietly says, "and so passes them. Dripping water patiently makes its way through the hardest stone. This is how your strength flows in and through and around your opponents."

I smile privately, thinking about the coincidence that the kwanjangnim's message for today would be about water, since that was all Ash could talk about last night. But while *Yu* teaches us patience and flow, one thing it doesn't explain is how to breathe in an airless environment. If the tunnels turn out to be a valid option, then we'll have to figure out how to get through them.

As far as I know, none of the five of us has ever been scuba diving. In fact, I've never even been snorkeling, except in the neighbor's pool when I was five, but that doesn't really count.

I settle on the bench and pull out my Link and ping Kelly to see if he's awake yet. It sends me straight to his message box, so he's either playing or still asleep.

"Sunbae," Kwanjangnim Rupert calls over at me, startling me out of my thoughts. He walks over and stands before me with his hands on his hips. I exit the app and slide the Link into my bag. I'll try again later or just stop by his house after I'm done here.

"Yes sir!" I shout, as I jump to my feet.

"You're early." He smiles knowingly. I have a reputation for being a late-sleeper.

"I wanted to get today's exercises out of the way, Kwanjangnim."

He gives me a strange look and asks, "What could be more important than your training?"

I quickly backtrack. "I mean, it looks like it's going to be another hot one today. I figured I'd beat the crowds."

"Is this the beginning of a new Jessie?"

The boy looks up from where he's stretching on the mat and his eyes widen. He's tall for his age, blond, big-boned, bordering on heavyset. He has this ruggedness about him, like he'd be a football or rugby player if they weren't illegal sports. He looks a little familiar, but I can't seem to place him. I think he might be in the grade below me, although I know that's not the real reason for my ignorance. Ashley's a grade below, too. The real truth is he's not part of our circle, our gang of gamers and hackers. I don't do much socializing with anyone outside of it. Not even with other hapkido students.

"Ready to spar?" Kwanjangnim asks me.

I nod. "Yes sir." I jump up and stand to one side so he can lead me onto the mat.

"Oh no, not me. Today I'll be talking it easy."

"Why?"

He groans. "I strained my back this morning."

Once more I glance over at the boy. "From sparring?" I can't imagine Master Rupert being injured by a lowly green belt.

"No," Kwanjangnim says. His laughter is thick and contagious. His face gets a little red. "I got hurt.... Actually, I strained it getting out of bed." He rubs his back and shrugs. "I guess I'm getting old. Either that or my mattress is."

We both enjoy another laugh before he adds something about going in to get his implant soon. It kills the moment, leaving us standing in an awkward silence before he gestures the boy over.

"This is Sunbae Jacob Espinosa," he says, introducing us. "Sunbae Jessica Daniels."

"Jake," the boy says, offering his hand. Meanwhile, I've bowed, so he withdraws it, even as I raise up and extend mine. Finally, we both clasp hands and bow awkwardly to each other. His grip feels weak, like he's consciously afraid of hurting me.

Rupert laughs at us and says, "Jake's new to the school. His forms are really pretty good. You two can warm up on each other, but for sparring today, no kicks, okay, Jess? Just hands, hits and holds. And try to take it easy on him. He'll be testing for his next belt in a week and we need him all in one piece."

"Bring it!" Jake says, slipping into a sparring stance. Rupert frowns, but I return the challenge with a growl.

"Keep it clean, guys!"

Despite the differences in our skill levels and the restriction on kicks, it turns out to be a good workout. Jake's quick and strong, almost as good as most of the red and black belts I'm used to sparring against. But he's also a bit top-heavy, and I'm clearly a lot more seasoned. After dropping him for the fifth or sixth time, I get him in an arm hold that he can't escape out of.

He calls it quits, saying he's got to leave, but just as my grip relaxes, he spins under me and wrenches my arm. The next thing I know, I'm lying on the floor with his knee on my back and my arm twisted away from me. I can't move.

"That was a cheap shot," I say between clenched teeth.

He lets go and stands up. "Sorry."

When I get up, I think I see a brief flash in his eyes, something powerful. I can't tell what it is. He looks away too quickly.

While I'm packing my gear, he comes over to talk to me. I wait for him to apologize. I'm still a little miffed by the unexpected throw, so I just grunt responses. That sort of poor sportsmanship isn't allowed in here, and if Kwanjangnim Rupert or any of the other trainers had seen what he'd done, they would've given Jake a severe tongue-lashing.

He tells me he's only been training for about ten months, and I tell him nobody gets as good as that in such a short time, which makes him pause. I might as well have called him a liar.

"I . . . I guess I'm a quick learner," he stutters. "How about you? How long have you been training?"

I give him a good long look before telling him I've been at it for eight years. "Off and on," I say, though it's not exactly the truth. I did miss one summer when Eric took us on a trip to Seattle after he got out of the Marines. "And I started in juniors."

He shakes his head and stares at me, a smile curling his lips.

"What's so funny?" I ask.

"I'm sorry. It's just that . . . ."

I narrow my eyes and wait for him to finish.

"I guess I was a little surprised to see you walk in this morning."

I stare at him. "Have we met before?"

"Um, no. But Ashley Evans talks about you all the time," he explains. "Says you have mad gaming skills. She was my science partner last year in chemistry lab. She's a jacker, right?"

"Jacker?"

"Game hacker. That's what the kids call her and others like her."

I think about this for a moment, then decide I actually like the term. Even though it doesn't apply to me specifically, it does describe the others quite well. "I just play. I don't hack."

He nods, tentatively, and looks around for something to say.

"I have to go," I tell him.

"I really enjoyed you this morning! The sparring, I mean. Not you. That is, you're really good."

"Are you hitting on me?"

He blushes.

"I already have a boyfriend."

His face reddens even more. He looks like he's about to choke. I smile. At least we're even now.

"Kidding," I tell him. "To be honest, though, if it ever came down to it, you'd probably kick his ass."

He laughs. I can see him relax. "And you could easily kick mine," he says.

"In a fair fight, maybe." He's got a good four inches on me and probably fifty pounds. And he is strong.

"I'm sorry about that move back there. The last dojo I was in didn't care too much about etiquette. It was all about skill and strength and speed and taking advantage of our opponents' weaknesses. That's one of the reasons why I transferred here."

"Don't sweat it," I say. "Just don't let it happen again."

Chapter Two

I ping Kelly again on my way out. He immediately connects this time. As I walk past the window I look in. Jake's just standing there watching me leave. I can't see his eyes because of the reflection, but something about the way he's staring makes me a little uncomfortable. It may be totally innocent, but I can't decide whether to feel threatened, creeped out or flattered by the attention.

" 'Sup, J?"

I hurry away, but I can feel his eyes on my back.

"On my way home from practice. Mind if I stop by?"

"Mom's here, but sure. I'm just hanging out, not really doing anything."

"Translation: trying to figure out a way to get past level eleven," I say.

He sighs and tells me I'm coldhearted. "So much for Micah's extra cheater lives. I'm lame. I'm just a lame gamer."

"Self-pity doesn't suit you, Kel."

"Nothing lamer than a poor-ass gamer like— *Wait a sec . . . . Yes! Woohoo!*"

"You're playing right now, aren't you? You're playing even as I'm talking to you."

" . . . maybe."

Frustration wavers on the verge of anger. I don't know what's going on between us, but lately it feels like he's slipping away. I don't want to lose him, and yet it feels like I am

"It's just the 2D version," he says, trying to placate me. "You know we don't have HG."

"Just save some of that energy for me," I say. It's a desperate move to distract him, make him pay more attention to me. I immediately feel guilty for being so needy, but not enough not to use my coup-de-gras: "I'm feeling frisky."

"Um, I did mention my mom's home, right?"

"Never stopped us before."

I can hear him exhale shakily into the Link, and it brings a smile to my face.

When I get to Kelly's house, his five-year-old brother Kyle answers the door. He gives me a big smile and a hug, which I enthusiastically return with change: an extra loud zerbit on his neck. He runs away giggling.

"Better watch it," I warn Kelly, when he wanders down from his room. "Looks like you've got some competition."

"What? Kyle? Robbing the cradle now, are you?"

"No one will ever replace Kyle," I answer. "Not even you. No, I mean at the dojang. There's this new kid. I sparred with him this morning. I think I embarrassed him when I suggested he was hitting on me."

"Was he?" Kelly asks.

"Easy there, cowboy," I reply, but even I'm not so sure what it really was that happened. "Jake couldn't land a real hit, much less a figurative one, unless I let him."

Did you? Let him, I mean."

"Really? Don't be like that, Kel"

He sighs. "So . . . Jake, huh? Do I know him?"

"Doubtful. He's a junior. Not a gamer or hacker. Seems Ash does, though. He was her science lab partner last year."

I take Kelly's arm and lead him back upstairs.

"Keep the door open," his mother yells up at us from the kitchen.

"Morning, Mrs. C," I shout back.

We keep the door open — barely — but we don't exactly behave. Even an open door doesn't stop us from getting in some serious make-out time. And it sort of makes things a lot more exciting, too, knowing someone could walk in on us at any moment.

By the time his mother calls for Kelly to come down a half hour later, my whole body's tingling and I feel like I'm about to explode. Kelly has this glazed look in his eyes. I don't know who's in more agony, him or me.

We straighten our disheveled clothes and hair before going downstairs.

"What are you kids up to today?" Mrs. Corben asks innocently.

"Going over to Micah's," Kelly answers. He looks over at me, sees the look on my face and shrugs.

If Mrs. C notices this, she doesn't say anything. Instead, she looks her son up and down and then says, "Walk over. You could use the exercise. You're starting to get a little flabby."

"Mom! I'm not getting flabby!"

"Mm hmm. And what exercise have you gotten lately? Outside of VR, I mean."

I stay out of this conversation. I know anything I say will just come off sounding suggestive in a way that would make me look slutty.

She throws him an apple from the bowl on the counter and tells him not to stay too long. "Your father'll be home early tonight and he wants to talk to you about colleges."

Kelly grunts.

After I drop my sparring gear off at home and get a quick shower, we head out to Micah's.

"He pinged your Link while you were in the bathroom," Kelly informs me. There's a dark look in his eyes. "Did you talk with him last night after we left or something?"

It's not like Kelly to be jealous of Micah, but after my teasing him this morning, I figure he's probably a bit more sensitive than usual. That's what the make-out session was supposed to take care of.

I shake my head and tell him about Ash's call during dinner.

Kelly grumbles. "This is all just a waste of time. You know that, don't you? An exercise in futility. There's a reason they sealed that place off, and I'm sure they didn't just do a half-assed job about it."

I shrug. "So what if you're right? Even if it turns out to be impossible, it still beats just sitting around watching you play *Zpocalypto* all the time."

"I don't play it all the time!"

"Dude, you're totally obsessed with it."

"I just want to pass this level is all. What's wrong with that?"

I squeeze his hand as I stop, swinging him around to look at me. "*Then* what, Kelly? Level thirteen? Fourteen? When does it stop?"

He gives me a resentful look.

I sigh with frustration. "Last year you told me you didn't just want to be a code jockey. You wanted to go to college and become something more. Why else would you suffer with those academic geeks in the college track at school instead of being in the trade track like the rest of us?"

He shrugs.

I'd feared that his entering the college track last year would put a strain on our relationship, since it meant we wouldn't get to see each other as much during school, but it actually didn't matter. It wasn't like we saw much of each other during classes anyway. The real strain actually started over the summer, feeling like a repeat of last year.

"Now look at you," I say. "All of a sudden you're eating and sleeping and drinking that stupid game! You were the one person that the rest of us looked to as a reminder that there's more to life than games and codes. But now it's like you're addicted."

"Me?" he exclaims, yanking his hand away from mine. "You're accusing *me* of being obsessed? You're the one who's obsessed. You and Reggie—"

"Reggie's just a friend, Kel!"

"—and all the others. How could you even consider going into Gameland?"

"It's not Gameland, Kelly, and you know it. Reggie didn't mean to say Gameland. It's just LI, and it's just for fun—"

"It's not just for fun! This is serious. Micah's all over it like flies on dog crap! Stupid Reggie for even bringing up such a dumb idea. He's had some bad ones in the past, but this one takes the cake."

"Stop screaming at me."

He raises his hands to his head and stumbles off like he's hurt or something. I suddenly just want to kick him, to send him sprawling, to knock some sense into his brain. But to do so would be to violate all the principles of discipline I've ever been taught in hapkido. We never attack out of spite or anger. We only fight to diffuse those emotions and to defend ourselves.

But the thing is, I know he's right. We are obsessed with games. All of us. And why shouldn't we be? Look at all the things my generation grew up with that we can't control: global warming, a fractured government that has pretty much given up doing anything useful, the Undead. Why wouldn't we want to escape into a world we can manipulate? The worst consequences in a game are having to go back to the beginning and starting all over again. You can't do that in real life. When you die, you just keep playing.

It's telling that we're most obsessed with games where we have to fight the dead, since what we most want is to live and feel. We want to *experience* life. But we can't. Our lives are so full of rules and restrictions. Nobody ever pushes us because pushing goes against everything we're taught. "Go to school," they drone. On and on like it's a mantra. "Become like everyone else." Sometimes it feels like we're just going through the motions.

That's why we play. It allows us to escape.

And the worst part about it? Games are such piss-poor substitutes for life — flat and two-dimensional, even in HG — that they only make us want more. We want to do something dramatic, something that we can feel. Like break into LI.

Kelly stomps off, leaving me behind. How could he not understand?

I sigh and follow along after him.

Chapter Three

Ashley is talking to Micah when we arrive in his basement. "Any hacker worth her salt," she's saying, "should be able to access the old government systems." She looks up and nods at us, then goes back to typing.

"What're you doing?" I ask.

Micah waves us over. "We're trying to get into the military's old computers in the Forbidden Zones on Long Island."

"How? Are they even still running?"

He shrugs. "That's what we're trying to figure out right now. Reggie thinks they probably kept them operating for non-essential functions like environmental control and such."

"Environmental control?" Kelly asks. The contempt is thick in his voice. He hasn't looked at me once since storming off, and it just makes me even angrier at him. "What the hell do they need that for? UIs don't need air conditioning."

Micah raises his hands. "Don't look at me. Ask Reg. This is his show. I'm just here to provide services."

"Looks like they're up and running," Ash chimes in. "I can see their identifiers — IP addresses, I believe they were once called. Hello, little computers, this is Granny knocking on your firewalls. Let me in, let me in. Ooh, what crude encryption you have!"

Kelly shakes his head in disgust.

Ashley's playful grin turns into a frown. "Micah? Does it seem like a lot of traffic's going through those nodes?"

Micah leans over. We all do, but it's scrolling too fast for me to make anything out. He shrugs.

"It's a lot of data for basic maintenance programs, but you know how inefficient the old codices were."

I grow bored of watching it. "Speaking of Reggie, where is he?"

"Yo."

I turn around just in time to see him coming out of the bathroom zipping up his fly. I roll my eyes. He smiles his shit-eating grin. Thankfully he doesn't say anything stupid, like, "I left you a present in there." I don't think I could bear his grade-school humor this morning.

"Okay, assuming you can find a way in," Kelly says, leaning over Ash, "wouldn't they have upgraded to iVZ?"

"The systems were put into place before ArcTech even existed," Micah explains. "I don't think they would've bothered with iVZ codex. Too much hardware to transfer over and convert."

"Exactly," Ashley agrees, nodding. Her fingers fly over the keyboard. Type scrolls madly across the screen. "Which means we're talking about accessing pre-Stream databases and programming. What they called the Internet way back when. Piece of cake."

"Which means," Reggie pipes in, "nobody's watching it anymore."

"We *hope* no one's watching it."

"Why bother?"

I remember talking to Grandpa about the internet age, which preceded the ArcTech systems that he helped put into place before he "retired." He was the commander of the Omegaman Forces, back when reanimation was first developed and zombies — initially called Zulus — were put under computer control using the L.I.N.C.s, which are similar to the latent individualized neuroleptic connections that all living citizens are supposed to get now. L.I.N.C.s are what connect us and our handheld Link devices to the Stream.

I reach my hand up to the back of my head and feel around until my fingers find the tiny scars. I got mine when I was three, even before it became mandatory. I remember Eric didn't want to get his. He argued that it was just another example of government intrusiveness, of thinking it knows what's best for us. But Grandpa convinced Mom and she signed the papers, so Eric had no choice. He was eleven.

They say the implants are there to prevent what happened during the outbreaks — so they can shut us down if we ever get infected — but it's pretty obvious the program has some serious flaws to it. How do you guarantee a hundred percent of the population is compliant? You can't. Look at Master Rupert: he's got to be in his fifties, and he still doesn't have his implant.

I lower my hand and say, "If it's pre-iVZ, then don't you need a physical uplink? There's no more wireless towers anymore, right?"

Grandpa had said that everything back in the first couple decades of the century either required a physical connection — which they called 'wired' because information was passed in the form of electrons through actual circuits — or radio waves — which they called 'wireless.' But all the wireless transmitters were disassembled years ago and replaced with EM towers. Electromagnetic signals are much more efficient and a trillion times more secure.

I remember him telling me how the old defcon management system was totally susceptible to hacking, and that it was a miracle nobody ever went in and triggered a bunch of missile launches. In fact, that's why ArcTech was first created, to design better, more secure computing systems. ArcTech's intralink VZ and the Stream replaced the Internet years ago and, along with it, the Cloud, which turned out to be a huge disaster. And although many have tried to hack into iVZ — including a few right here in this very room — nobody's ever been able to do it. The encryption is just too good.

Micah holds up a cable, which I can see he's spliced into the guts of yet another piece of equipment, which I immediately recognize as highly illegal: an old tablet computer. "What's the saying about necessity?" he asks.

"It's the mother fucker of invention," Reggie replies, and he and Micah slap palms.

Ashley suddenly yelps. She reaches over and yanks out the wires.

"Hey," Micah cries, but then we all see the look on her face.

"There was some fishy code flashing by in there. I think it was trying to track us so I severed the connection."

Getting caught hacking a government system — even an old one — would get us into serious trouble, enough to probably add six or seven years to our Life Service commitment.

It reminds me of the close call we had a couple weeks ago when Ash and Micah tried hacking into the VR part of *The Game*. They'd spent a solid three days down here, barely sleeping, feeding on nothing but Red Bull and Little Caesar's pizza. They said it was a hundred times harder than anything they'd tried before. Heck, maybe a million times.

Most of the programming developed and used by ArcWare is open source. Even so, they always embed a few black boxes within the games to keep things interesting, cryptic code that somehow adapts the game to a player's habits and skill level. Gamers and hackers alike love that they do it. Otherwise, what would be the fun in playing or hacking into them?

Not *The Game*, though. That's a whole different animal. *The Game* is protected by an ArcWare-developed code called iVZ, short for "intralink virtual zeality." It's got one of the most sophisticated firewalls any of us has ever seen, and a proprietary base code that none of us could ever hope to break. It's light years beyond military grade. In fact, iVZ powers the government. Hack into *The Game* and you'd practically have the tools needed to hack into the national defense system.

It was Ashley who first proposed the idea to crack *The Game*. She'd built this crude translator for ArcWare programs. That's how we found their back door. How she accomplished that is beyond me — I'm not a hacker like she and Micah and Reggie are. She's hacked into more of ArcWare's black boxes than anyone I know. She said she used what she salvaged as sort of a Rosetta Stone to come up with her translator, a frankensteinian piece of software built from bits and pieces of scavenged code.

"It's a heuristic program," she tried to explain to me, apparently oblivious to the fact that my eyes were quickly glazing over. I prefer nascent coding, creating programs. And I stick to the standard languages, like andro, Khartoum-four and MesmerZ. Going in specifically to crack a program isn't my idea of fun.

"Heuristic means it teaches itself," she went on. Of course I knew what heuristic meant, but I didn't bother to correct her. "The program essentially runs on a loop of testing, evaluating, refining and retesting, becoming better and better as it ages."

Whatever. I never, ever thought it would work.

But it did. Sort of. Between her and Micah's mad coding abilities, they got as far as copying the software's architecture before the program shut them out. Architecture is Micah's specialty. He loves thinking about game structure and could stare at it all day long, drooling like a puppy at how clever some of the programmers can be.

I remember Ash pinged everyone when they made the breakthrough. We all went running over.

I got there just in time to see Micah's screens lighting up with error messages Then everything went totally ape-shit.

"Yo, there's suicide switches everywhere, y'all!" he shouted. We stood in awe and watched, making sure to stand out of the way as he hammered at his keyboard. It was fun just watching him. He and Ash were hopping from console to console, the whole time shouting at the top of their lungs. Then: "Not another— " Micah screamed. "No, no! Aw, shee-it!"

Everything went blank. The game had locked them out. Wouldn't even let them log in with new fake identities, blocking us all out, in fact. It was as if it suddenly knew everything about us, could track us even if we jumped Streams. It was a huge disappointment, of course. We'd gotten a glimpse inside *The Game*, but we'd almost gotten caught, too.

"Easy peasy," Ashley says, as she holds up the tablet in triumph.

"You got the maps?" Micah asks. "Lady, I could just kiss you!"

"You wouldn't be able handle it. You'd spontaneously combust!"

"What maps?" Kelly asks, impatiently.

"The tunnels," I say. "Weren't you even listening this morning when I told you about it?" I know I'm just taking out my frustration on Kelly, but I can't seem to help myself.

He frowns at me, then shakes his head and repeats the question.

Ash holds up the disemboweled tablet. What we see on the pixilated screen is an old drawing of the transportation system of Long Island. She points to a pair of lines connecting lower and eastern Manhattan to LI. The first is labeled BROOKLYN BATTERY TUNNEL. The second, QUEENS MIDTOWN TUNNEL.

"Schematics are embedded. Which one do you want to check out first?"

We all look at each other without speaking. What we're seeing is highly illegal to possess, much less study. Then we're all speaking at the same time.

"The Queens," Kelly announces, when the rest of us have quieted down. "Let's look at that one first."

Ash opens the embedded file and begins to read:

"*Opened in 1940, the Queens-Midtown tunnel connects the Borough of Queens on Long Island with the Borough of Manhattan. It consists of twin tubes carrying four traffic lanes and is 6,414 feet long.*"

"Over a mile," I murmur. I don't know what I'd been expecting, but it certainly isn't something quite as long as that. "How're we going to get through something a mile long and filled with water?"

"Scuba," Reggie says.

"Whoa!" Kelly turns to Reg. "Getting a little ahead of ourselves, aren't we? Nobody here knows how to scuba dive. Besides, we don't even know if the tunnel's still accessible."

"Yeah, well, the other tunnel's even longer," Ash says, busily reciting facts from the other file. As if it makes any difference. One mile or ten, scuba gear or not, Kelly's right. If the tunnels aren't open, we might as well be talking about swimming through concrete.

By rights, they should all be filled. Or at least gated. And for all we know, they could be caved in. It's a hundred years old, for chrissake. And despite Ash's assurances to me last night, I still seriously doubt they'd just leave the openings unblocked.

Micah asks where the Manhattan opening for the Queens tunnel is.

Ashley taps the screen. "The old midtown," she says. "Between what used to be East 34th and 35th Streets." She opens another file. Nods. "Yep. It's totally underwater."

"Okay, then," Kelly says, holding up a gaming controller. "Now that that's resolved, how about we—"

"Check it out?" Reggie says, straightening up. "Good idea. I mean, we won't know for sure what it looks like unless we see it for ourselves, right?"

Ash turns to me. "Did you bring it?" she asks.

I nod and pat my Link. "Uploaded it last night, after Eric went to bed." Kelly frowns at me like I've betrayed him.

"Woohoo!" Reggie shouts. "Road trip!"

Chapter Four

The five of us pile into Micah's beat up old Ford. It's so ancient that it even has a docking station for the old Apple iCorp storage devices rather than getting music from the Stream.

Micah drives. Reggie takes shotgun. The rest of us sit in back. We head down Route 95, which is the quickest way to Manhattan, even though it means having to pass through about a half dozen checkpoints, including the ones at each interstate border crossing.

After about twenty minutes, we pass through the first. The guard looks bored. He scans our Links and doesn't speak.

I see the abandoned Teterboro Airport off in the distance. The moss-covered hangars poke out of the water like giant eggs that never hatched.

Finally the guard waves us through. He doesn't even bother to ask where we're going.

"There's the Meadowlands," Reggie says, pointing off to the side a minute later, and I think about how the old football stadium looks like a giant concrete nest to go with the eggs.

"Don't you mean the Swamplands?" Ashley remarks, making us all laugh.

This leads to a discussion by the boys about the banned sport of football, with Reggie arguing that they should bring it back and Kelly saying it was a brutal sport that has no place in our world today. I want to slap him and ask what place zombies have in our world, and isn't the television show, *Survivalist*, or *The Game*, on which it's based, just as brutal? But I don't. I feel like we're already treading on thin ice today.

We come to another checkpoint just before crossing the new elevated bridge that will take us into Manhattan. Here, the guard asks us where we're going and what we're doing. "School project," Ash pipes up. The guard gives us a doubtful look and she quickly adds, "Summer school."

"College track," he says, sneering, but he scans our Links, then asks if we all have implants. After recording our IDs, he lets us pass.

"School?" Reggie asks, once we're clear. "Really? That's the best you could come up with?"

Ash laughs and shrugs and says she just got nervous. "You know me. I don't think well under pressure."

Soon we're zooming right over Central Park. Looking down is enough to make anyone queasy, but Reggie sticks his head out the window and howls like a wolf. The wind whips the spit from his lips, and I'm suddenly glad I'm sitting in the middle of the backseat. If anyone gets sprayed, it's

Kelly, but he doesn't say anything. He just sits there glowering out the window.

I elbow him and give him a smile. He sighs and offers me a half of a smile back, his way of forgiving me. He relaxes, resting a little more of his weight against me. For his reward, I give him a kiss on the cheek.

"Get a room, lovebirds," Ashley groans. But of course, this just makes us laugh and want to do it some more.

I'm practically sitting on Kelly's lap when the road curves right and begins its gentle decline toward south Manhattan.

"Another checkpoint," Micah announces. "I quickly plop back into my seat, wiping my lips with the back of my hand. I reach down and squeeze Kelly's thigh and he nearly jumps through the roof of the car. I can't tell if he's so tense because of me or because we're getting closer to LI.

And we are close. I can smell the ocean. Water surrounds us all around, canals wending their way through and around the old skyscrapers, most of them abandoned now, crumbling. It's our own version of Italy's Venice. Of course, the real Venice is long gone now, buried under thirty feet of Mediterranean Sea years before I was even born. A diver's paradise.

Not that any of us'll ever get to see it.

We pull up at the checkpoint and this guard, after giving Micah's car a good looking over, flatly tells us no access. "This is a commercial district," he states.

Ash points to me and says I have a permit. I flash him my Link with Eric's permit on it and he inspects it for minute before handing it back. "Remember the curfew," he says. We all nod dutifully and promise to be out of New York long before dusk.

Despite all the restrictions and the hassles of the checkpoints, the roads are crowded with business people. So are the waterways. Water taxis ferry people around, drawing white trails in the deep blue. Despite all the flood damage on this side of the East River, despite the proximity of LI, Manhattan still somehow manages to be a bustling city. It's still the financial center of the universe, even though New Merica has essentially isolated itself from the rest of the world.

But then, every so often, I catch a glimpse of the stark gray walls of LI rising up across the water, looking like a giant alien ship or a prison.

How do these people work here every day knowing what lies on the other side of the river, not two miles away? How can they look out over it and see that wall every day and not give it a second thought? It's so close. Or do they just pretend it's not there?

After the first outbreak, thirteen years ago, the military went in to control the Infected Undead and evacuate the living. Certain parts were declared disaster areas. They set up barriers and controlled access, preventing people from moving back in. These eventually became known as Forbidden Zones. But the zones kept growing, getting larger and larger, spreading out until, eventually, they began to connect with each other. The flooded Wastelands were now truly lost, leaving only the higher points of land free, isolated pockets on which the last stubborn islanders remained.

The government said sealing the island off was for the protection of the living from the Undead. But Eric once told me the truth was quite different. It was to protect the Undead from illegal poaching by people who didn't think it was right to let the Undead roam free.

"The government considers zombies assets," he told me. "Even those without implants. After all, each one could take the place of a living soldier who won't have to go into combat."

But nobody knows if anyone ever went in and implanted any of the IUs. It seems unlikely.

Congress passed the Life Service Law almost ten years ago. Now, every single person is legally considered government property after death, not just the ex-criminals, and not just the ones that made up the Omegaman Forces. Although the law has since been challenged several times in the Supreme Court, the politicians and the judges are too spineless to strike the thing down. And, honestly? Nobody except a few rights activists really wants to. We may not like the idea that we'll become one of the Undead someday and have to pay our dues to the government, but it's better than going back to the old ways, when living people fought wars and cleaned sewers.

The road finally reaches its lowest point, which is still about sixty feet above water level. It's where the experts say sea level will be when all the arctic ice finally finishes melting. They say that won't happen for another hundred years, but that's what they said forty years ago before the first major ice shelf broke off and raised sea levels by thirty feet.

"Times Square," Micah calls out. We all look to the right. The place is a dump, abandoned and disintegrating. "We should be just about parallel with the tunnel now. A few more blocks to the south and we'll be there."

Traffic has thinned out quickly and is now almost nonexistent. We come to one last checkpoint. Here, the guard is all business. We sit silently as he checks our Links. He takes each one and scans it, then does the same with each of us, making sure our Links match our implants. He spends a lot of time with Micah's until, finally, Micah asks for his Link back. He messes with it for a moment before returning it to the guard.

"It's been having problems lately," Micah says. "I think it's time for an upgrade."

The guard frowns for a moment, stares at the screen, then at Micah. His jaw clenches and he takes in a deep breath.

"This is an inner zone," he says. "What's your reason for coming here?"

This time, when Ashley explains that it's an extra-credit project for summer school, he just stands there tapping his thumb on his own Link, waiting for us to come clean.

"We swear it," Ashley insists. "It's part of our community service commitment."

"And the NCD permit? How does that fit in?"

"My brother works for the department," I explain. "Eric Daniels? You probably know him."

The guard just stares.

"We're doing a survey in conjunction with the police department. It's on...."

"Potential sources of outbreak transmission," Kelly says.

The guard sighs. "Zombie freaks. Okay. Just don't go anywhere restricted. Heed the signs. Don't get in any trouble. Fines are doubled in an inner zone. And remember the curfew."

We all breathe a sigh of relief as he waves us through.

"Outbreak transmission?" I ask Kelly, once we've pulled away.

"I had to say something. You guys were totally boffing it back there."

"Thanks," I say. "I knew there was a reason I kept you around." I lean over and grab his face for another kiss.

"Aw, sheesh," Ash complains. "Not again."

We stop at a traffic light, and dutifully wait for it to change, even though there are no other cars around. I glance down and see an empty water taxi stand just outside the old Grand Central Station. A bunch of obsolete train cars had been hoisted onto the rooftop platform and converted into high-priced restaurants and hotels. They all stand empty and rundown now. Grass sprouts out of every corner and crack.

"Take a left here," Reggie says, checking his Link. Micah turns on his blinker, making Reggie snort and shake his head.

After a few more minutes, the buildings thin out, become shorter, squatter. Then the vista suddenly opens up. We all exhale as one as the dull gray desert of the East River spreads out before us, as if it's the most wondrous thing we've ever seen. In truth, it kind of scares me.

"According to my Link," Micah says, "we're almost where the opening should be. Just a few hundred feet ."

We all look down, but of course there's nothing to see. It's not like there's going to be a blinking sign pointing the way: *Access to illegal tunnel to LI.*

Micah pulls into a deserted parking structure and stops the car. We're the only ones there. We get out and follow Reggie, who's got his Link held in front of him like a divining rod. After a few minutes, we reach the end of building and he points out about a hundred feet. "Should be right about . . . there."

All I can see is a big gaping pool of water, roughly three hundred feet wide. It stretches out for at least a quarter mile until we lose it in the distance.

"Look! You can see the sides of the entrance ramp there!" He thrusts his arm to the right and, sure enough, we can see part of the ancient roadway surfacing a few hundred feet away, looking like the tongue of sleeping beast hanging out of its wet mouth. He swings his hand in the opposite direction and adds, "So, that walkway there should be the old overpass covering the mouth of the tunnel."

Ashley pulls out the reassembled tablet and boots it up. The thirty or so seconds it takes feels like forever. Old tech, I think to myself. How did people ever have the patience for it? Makes me realize how lucky we are to be constantly connected, constantly on.

When it's ready, Ash opens an old photograph of the tunnel entrance and we all crowd around to see. The resolution's horrible, but now we can see the familiar landmarks. The walls look to have been constructed from hewn stone. The tunnel opening stops approximately twelve or fifteen feet below the top of the overpass. Now, only the upper five or six feet of the structure are above water, but there's a muddy high tide line just below the surface of the road.

"Must be connected to the river here," I say.

Micah nods. "Half of lower Manhattan is."

There's no water in the photo, of course, just ancient cars going into and out of the tunnel.

"Shall we try and get closer?" Micah says, extending his elbow to Ashley.

She twines her arm around his and answers, "We shall." They're acting like this is all a game. I'm actually feeling a little giddy myself.

Micah, Kel and I follow. We go down a couple flights of stairs and reach a sidewalk that surrounds the building. To the left is a loading platform for watercraft. It's probably less than fifteen years old, but it looks much older. To the right, the walkway arches out past the edge of the building.

Kelly holds back. "Seriously, guys? What are we doing? So we get closer. Then what? How're you going to know if the tunnel's open?"

"We draw straws," I joke. "The winner gets to go swimming."

They all look at me. But I shake my head. "Except me. I left my medicine at home."

It's got to be one of the lamest things I've said in a long time, and a really bad excuse to boot. Reggie laughs at me. He shakes his head and says, "Nobody's going swimming. We're just scoping things out today. I just want to see how close we can get. Next time we come back — tomorrow, maybe, or Saturday — we'll be better prepared."

"Prepared for what?"

Reggie raises his eyebrows at Kelly. "Duh. A little exploratory work."

This clearly doesn't please Kelly. He drags his feet while the others follow Reggie. I lag behind to walk with him.

"What's this all about?" I ask him, when the others are out of earshot. "Why are you acting like this all of a sudden?"

"What do you mean, Jess?"

I roll my eyes. I don't know what else to say that won't make things worse, so we walk along for a few more minutes without speaking. Then he elbows me and gives me a wry smile. "I can't believe you forgot your inhaler. Tsk, tsk. What's the Colonel going to say?"

"Grandpa doesn't know." I shove him playfully. "And he doesn't need to find out, either."

I've used the inhaler my entire life. I'm supposed to carry it around with me all the time and puff on it three times a day, so it's become almost habit. But I do forget on occasion, and when my grandfather finds out, he gets all OCD about it and interrogates me for like the next week. *How am I feeling? Have I taken all three doses? Do I feel sick?*

Most of the time I can honestly answer that I'm following my regimen, but sometimes I forget. Like today. I'd forgotten to take it out of my gear bag this morning and left it at home.

I shrug and tell Kelly that we'll be back soon and I'll just take a dose then. "It's not like I'm going to drop dead if I don't. It's just an immunity booster."

The truth of the matter is, I'm not exactly sure what it's supposed to do. I've always been told by the doctors that it's to help stave off infections, but they've never really clearly explained what's wrong with me that I should need it.

Sometimes I hate having the inhaler; it makes me feel weak and vulnerable. Other times, though, I'm glad for it. Like, for example, whenever I want to get out of having to do gym class, I just hold it up and complain that I feel like I'm coming down with something. It's a lot easier and less embarrassing than saying I'm having menstrual cramps.

We reach the end of the walkway. Ash and Micah have stopped and are leaning out across the railing. They're looking down into the darkness below us. "The opening's right here," Ash says, even though there's no way she can possibly see it. "Does it look to you like it's open?"

I look down, but it's too dark and the sunlight keeps bouncing up and into my eyes. I try to lean further over. Before I realize what's happening, there's a flash of color off to the side, a splash, and water sprays up at us. I stumble back gasping and wiping it from my face.

"What the hell was that?"

"Dude!" Reggie exclaims. He's got a huge smile plastered over his face. "Kelly is what happened, that's what. Crazy mother fucker. What'd you say to him to make him jump, Jessie?"

"Kelly?" I shout, running back over to the railing and looking down, but there's nothing to see. "I didn't tell him to jump, you idiot!"

This shuts him up.

"Don't just stand there! Do something!"

But nobody moves. Nobody wants to jump into that murky water. We all wait and count the seconds.

Thirty heartbeats pass. Then forty . . . . Fifty . . . .

Sixty.

"Kelly," I moan.

A minute and half is gone just like that and now I'm really starting to get scared. Ashley's eyes have grown wide, too. She's got her fingertips in her mouth. She's chewing on her nails. Even Reggie and Micah are beginning to look a little nervous.

"It's barely two minutes," Micah says. "I can hold my breath for two minutes. Hell, I could hold it for three if I needed to."

But all I can think is that it's Kelly we're talking about, not Micah. Kelly's not conditioned for holding his breath.

"How long?" I ask. Nobody answers. "*How long!*"

"Three minutes."

"Kelly!" I scream. "*Kelly!*"

Then everyone's yelling, shouting his name. Reggie's peeling off his shirt and getting ready to climb onto the railing. Micah begins to kick off his shoes. But we're all interrupted by a shrill whistle coming from man in a dark green uniform. He starts running toward us.

"You there! You kids! Stop right there! There's no swimming here."

Reggie's standing on the first rail, leaning his knees against the top rung, looking like he's going to jump in anyway. The cop blows his whistle even harder and waves his EM pistol frantically at us. Now he's about a hundred feet away.

"Our friend fell in!" Micah shouts. "He fell in! It was an accident. We need help!"

The cop reaches us, his feet slapping the sidewalk. He's panting and I'm sobbing by then. So's Ashley.

"Our friend fell in! We have to save him!"

"You can't go down there," the cop says. He's an older man, graying at the temples. His face is rough and scarred. He shoves his pistol back in its holster but keeps his hand on it. "It's dangerous. Bad currents. Can't you see the signs?" He points.

"But our friend—"

Just then there's a watery gasp from below us and Kelly's head pops up. His face is blue and his eyes are bulging. He scrambles to grab onto something, but the edge of the overpass is too far out of reach. The cop bends down under the railing. He leans over and extends his baton.

"Grab onto this, young man."

Kelly gets a hold of the baton, but he's too weak to pull himself up. Reggie joins the cop. He reaches down and grabs both of Kelly's arms and he lifts him out of the water like he's nothing but a stack of wet laundry. Kelly shoots up and manages to grab the lowest rail.

Reggie slips out from underneath and quickly repositions himself over the railing. "Hold on!" Kelly hurtles over it and smacks down on the walkway, where he collapses in a wet, shivering heap.

I rush over and wrap my arms around him. He places his face in the crook of my neck. His skin is cold and there's a scratch on his cheek that's just starting to pink up with fresh blood. I notice he's hiding it from the cop.

"There's no swimming here," the officer repeats. "I could have you arrested." He gives us a stern look and keeps it on us a few seconds longer than necessary. We all know what that means. An arrest like this would go on our permanent record and add time to our LSC, time that would, without a doubt, get front-ended.

He sighs and shakes his head. "What are you kids doing down here anyway? This is no place for young folks like you to be. You should be at home enjoying the summer break."

We all look around at each other. Finally, Ashley manages to say, "School project?"

The cop snorts. "Right, like I'm supposed to believe that."

"We were just looking for some privacy," Reggie says. He sidles up to Ash and wraps his arms around her.

The cop sizes them up for a moment — giant Reggie and diminutive Ash — then he looks at me and Kelly. Finally his gaze settles on Micah and we can all see that he's figuring out the math. His eyes flit around, as if he expects to see another person to be hiding somewhere.

But he just shakes his head again and tells us the next time he comes by we had better be gone. "This is a class B zone," he tells us. "Only authorized individuals are allowed in here. It's not a . . . . It's not a motel."

He turns on his heels and walks away, much to our surprise. He doesn't even bother to scan us.

"Class B?" Reggie whispers in disbelief. "Man, we are so lucky he didn't bust us."

Class A would be the East River, of course. The penalty for trespassing there wouldn't be arrest or LSC years. It would be vaporization by one of the mines.

When the sound of the cop's shoes on the pavement fades away, I turn back to Kelly and shake him. "What the hell were you thinking jumping in there? You almost drowned!"

He slowly raises his eyes, but he doesn't look at me. It's Reggie he stares at, his eyes dark and penetrating. "Well, Reg, you wanted to know if the tunnel's open. I got your answer." He takes in a shuddering breath and looks at the rest of us.

"Blocked?" Reggie asks.

Kelly shakes his head. He shivers again and says, "Open. All the way through."

Chapter Five

"How do you know?" Ashley asks. "How could you possibly know it's open all the way through?"

"Currents," Kelly replies, pushing me away a little. I think about the cop mentioning currents and realize he's right. In order for there to be currents, the tunnel must be open.

"They're actually pretty strong down there. It was almost like getting sucked into a drain. Lucky for me, the current was pushing me back out, otherwise . . . ." He doesn't finish. He doesn't need to.

He coughs, spits. "I ended up grabbing onto some old wiring or something and pulling myself along the ceiling. I went as far as I could before I ran out of air and needed to turn around."

"That was some crazy-ass shit, man," Reggie says.

Kelly locks eyes with Reg and doesn't answer. After a few seconds pass, he combs his dripping hair away from his forehead with his fingers.

"I thought I'd just let the current push me back out, but then my shirt got caught on something." He lifts his arm to show us the tear under his left sleeve.

I don't know why the next thought pops into my head, but suddenly I wonder if the cop happened to notice the rip. Why that would matter I don't know, but the whole encounter strikes me as odd, forced. Why would he just take off like that without even scanning us? And what does Kelly know that he'd want to hide the scratch from him?

Kelly laughs weakly and shakes his head. "I sort of panicked, thinking it was one of those sewer gators you always hear about."

"Urban myth," Micah says.

"I guess I freaked out. I lost my air. I tried to kick. Whatever it was holding me tore away. I felt my shirt rip and the next thing I knew, I was shooting back out with the current. Good thing too, because I don't think I'd have made it out if it was even another second or two. I'd probably have inhaled a gallon of water and sunk straight to the bottom."

"What do you think it was?" Ashley asks. "That snagged you, I mean." She has this worried look on her face. We can all see what she's thinking, but nobody wants to say it.

Kelly shrugs. "Loose panel or something. Maybe a jammed log or a pipe. I don't know. It was too dark to see. There's got to be a ton of crap washed down into there, just not enough to block the flow entirely. The current's definitely strong enough to move a lot of water, so there's got to be spaces wide enough for a person to swim through."

I lean back and study Kelly and wonder why he's suddenly stopped being so resistant.

"Or maybe it was a zombie," Reggie jokes.

He suddenly laughs and slaps Kelly on the back and makes appreciative sounding noises. "Just kidding, brah. But, man, that was totally off-the-wall, what you did."

Everyone nods, but I'm still furious.

"Why?" I scream at him. "You're the last person I would've expected to do something stupid like jump into the river!"

"It's not the riv— "

"I don't care what it is! You could've drowned."

He shrugs and sighs. "Maybe that's why I did it," he says, studying my face. "I don't know. Maybe I just realized that you're always right about stuff and I'm wrong and such a stick in the mud all the time. I just figured I'd see for myself."

"You could've lied about it," Micah quietly says. "You could've told us it was gated or something. We wouldn't have known any better."

"Believe me, I thought about it. But while I was struggling to untangle myself, I don't know, I guess I just thought, *really?*" He looks at Reggie. "I still think it's a bad idea, though. Nothing changed my mind about that."

Reggie shakes his head.

"Besides," Kelly goes on, "there's the other tunnel, the Brooklyn Battery. If I told you this one was blocked, knowing you guys, we'd just end up going over there and checking that one out. Am I right?"

A couple of us shrug and murmur our agreement.

"Guys?" Ashley says, interrupting the boys. "I hate to break up this little discussion, but maybe it's time we cleared out of here. I don't know if that cop was serious, but I don't want to find out. He said he'd be back, but he didn't say when."

Reggie and Micah help pull us to our feet. Despite the warmth of the day, Kelly is still shivering. The scratch on his cheek has stopped bleeding, but now it's puckered out white and angry-looking on his pale face. He lifts his shoulder to wipe it away, wincing, and a fresh thin line of blood appears.

"Don't do that," I tell him. "You'll only make it worse."

"How'd it happen?" Micah asks as we walk back to the car.

Kelly shrugs. "Like I said, it was dark. Whatever it was that snagged my shirt scratched my face too, I guess."

I take a closer look. There are three parallel scrapes, each separated from the other by about a half inch. They look like claw marks. Only the middle one is deep enough to break the skin. "Just make sure you put some antibiotic on it when we get back," I say.

"Yes, Mom," they all chorus.

I frown at them. "Hey, it may not be the East River *per se*, but it's still pretty nasty water."

Chapter Six

I wasn't worried about Kelly getting some nasty bacterial infection. I was worried about him coming down with something worse.

Ash's grandmother, Junie, used to joke about how, when she was my age, having unprotected sex could kill you. She passed away last year, quite unexpectedly. She could remember a time before the implants, before zombies. Back when diseases like AIDS and diabetes and cancer worried people. She'd laugh her bitter laugh because she knew things are a lot worse now, when there are diseases that don't just kill you, but raise you back up again.

"I hope they put me into *The Game*," she started saying to us, shortly before she died.

"Don't joke about it," Ashley told her.

"I'm serious, girl." Of course, we all knew it was highly unlikely she'd get her wish. Only the freshest and fittest of the recently deceased ever get recruited to be Players. "And think of the money it would bring the family."

"We don't need the money," Ash told her. But even I knew that wasn't true.

"But that's not why."

"Then why, G-ma? You know the lifespan of a game zombie is only a few weeks. Months at best, depending on your Operator." She shuddered; I knew she was remembering some of the scenes we'd watched on *Survivalist*.

"What they're made to do in *The Game* can be pretty brutal."

"I've seen that program, dear. I know. That's why I think it would be better. I'd rather spend my Life Service commitment doing that." G-ma Junie closed her eyes then and sighed, nodding. "A few brutal weeks. Who cares? I won't even know because I'll be dead. And if I'm dead, I want to be *dead* dead, not standing in some remote border outpost as a deterrent to trespassers or strapped to a bomb in Mexico. I just want to be laid to rest."

Of course, nobody gets 'laid to rest' anymore. They don't do burials. Everyone gets incinerated. *After* their LSC is completed.

Since her G-ma's death, Ashley has been talking more and more like that, too. "I'd rather just go quickly in *The Game*, even if it's to act out some sick fantasy of some sick rich fuck. Better that than be put to work cleaning sewers for three years or pulling guard duty. Although getting blown up would be a quick way to go, don't you think? I could be an Omega."

I remember once how Eric told me we probably won't have to worry about reaching our LSC age.

I knew he wasn't talking about a cure, or a change in the laws. He was talking about another outbreak happening, a real bad one. Global in reach, total in nature. An outbreak that wouldn't be quelled like the others.

There wouldn't be anyone left to quell it.

Chapter Seven

Kelly's clothes have stopped dripping by the time we get back to the car. We stop and wait for him to dump the water out of his shoes and wring his socks and shirt out. While we do, we see the cop from earlier walking past us down below. He's clearly checking to make sure we're gone, but he doesn't look up, so he doesn't see us.

Micah complains about his seat getting wet, so we just hang around and talk about nothing much while Kelly dries off some more.

"Do you really think we could do it?" Ash asks. "Do you think we could actually get to LI?"

I look out in the direction of Long Island, past the edge of the parking structure, out past the tunnel opening. I can't actually see it because there's another building in the way, but I can feel it out there. I shrug. Nobody answers.

Micah and Ash eventually drift away with their heads bent over the tablet. Reggie seems uncomfortable around us, so he trails along after them.

I turn to Kelly and smack him on the arm. "You scared the crap out of me, Kelly Corben."

He inhales, clears his throat. "I didn't jump, Jess."

"What? You fell?"

"I was pushed, Jessie. Somebody pushed me. I'm pretty sure it was Reg."

"He wouldn't do something like that!"

"How can you be so sure?"

"He's your friend, Kelly. *Our* friend. He's not— "

Kelly wraps his goose-fleshed arms around me and I squirm from the coldness of his skin and his clamminess, but he holds me ever tighter and won't let go. "Maybe you're right," he says. "Maybe I just slipped."

But he doesn't sound at all convinced. He sounds like he's humoring me. But I'm not amused. I give him another long, hard look.

He closes his eyes and leans his head back against the wall. I want to smack him again, but how can I? Something deep down inside of me knows what he said is possible. He and Reg have always been competitive. Micah's always been the alpha male in our gamers' club. The other two accepted that long ago, leaving open the question of who was second.

Boys! I think. Why'd it always have to be about power?

Thankfully, Micah returns a moment later. He asks where Ashley and Reggie are. He's ready to leave.

"I thought they were with you."

He shakes his head. We're all thinking the same thing.

"Idle hands do the devil's work," he mutters, rolling his eyes. "I wonder where Reggie's hands are idling right about now." He holds them out, illustrating exactly what he means so there's no question.

"That's disgusting! We're in a parking garage."

He laughs as he opens the car door and leans in to push on the horn. I stifle the urge to tell him to stop. He doesn't even seem to care that we're not supposed to be here.

"Ash!" he shouts. His voice echoes in the otherwise empty structure. "Reg! Come on, you pervs. Time to go!"

Two or three minutes later, the pair comes jogging over. Ashley's face is flushed, and Reggie's got his usual smile plastered on his face. Before any of us can say anything or tease them, Ash frowns at us and says, "Don't even think it. We kept our clothes on. We were just doing a little scouting."

We get back into the car. Kelly sits in the front this time, since he's still damp and nobody wants to sit next to someone who smells swampy. Ashley gets the hump this time in back, between me and Reg. I sit behind Micah, but I study Reggie's face for any indication he did what Kelly says he did. But there's nothing there.

"The cop makes a regular pass," Ashley says after we're back on the road. "We watched him. He does a circuit of some kind. It looks like it takes him almost exactly sixty minutes to do it."

I give her a questioning look.

"And what did you guys do?" she asks me, pretending to act all innocent.

"Not much," I say, but I steal another glance at Reg. He looks over at me, the same inquiring look on his face as Ash's. It's impossible to read him.

Kelly scratches his head. "Doesn't it seem strange to you that there'd be a cop patrolling? On foot? I mean, why? Nobody's going to be wandering around down there. The place is deserted."

"*We* were."

Micah's shoulders lift and fall as he drives, but he keeps his eyes on the road. Kelly frowns. The question remains unanswered, though not forgotten. It's just that none of us knows if there is an answer.

After that, the conversation drifts. We pass through the checkpoints and the guards don't even bother to scan our Links. Going out is a hell of a lot easier than going in. One guard checks the trunk of the car, but that's the most any of them does. Does he think we're carrying illegal contraband or something?

Micah drops me and Kelly off at my house. Nobody's home, so we take a risk and jump into the shower together while Kelly's clothes get washed.

We begin soaping each other down, but as much as I want to mess around, it's clear Kelly's mind is anywhere but on sex. We quickly rinse and towel off. I throw the clothes into the dryer while Kelly sits in my room wrapped in a towel and my robe.

"You look cute," I tell him. He looks over distractedly and turns back to his Link. I go over and peek over his shoulder. "What are you doing?"

"Looking up whatever I can find out about LI. You know, history and stuff."

"You know nothing that's on the public Streams is reliable."

He nods. "Still, better to be prepared."

"I thought . . . ."

"What?" He looks up expectantly.

"Nothing."

The sanctioned history claims that the wall was first built around the island to stop the spread of infections. But the outbreaks kept on happening anyway. The government says it's because of sabotage, but that's not what most people believe. Some of the more recent outbreaks have been as far away as Seattle and Los Angeles. But they don't get much play on Media. They've been small, a few hundred cases at the most, and quite easily contained. In fact, there was nothing like the panics caused by the ones on the East Coast. It's like we've gotten used to them happening. Nobody even bothers to be worried anymore. We've all become desensitized.

There are a ton of theories circulating about how the outbreaks happen. Some people believe they're caused by mosquito-borne transmission. There's rumors that the original genes used to make the first Zulus came from a virus called dengue, which was spread by mosquitoes.

Grandpa says that's impossible. He says dengue was eradicated after the plague of 2012 by this scientist who blocked the virus' ability to replicate inside mosquitoes. The scientist's name was Stephen something — Archangel, maybe — I can't remember, and there's nothing about it on the Stream.

Other people think the infection can be transmitted through the water. That's why I didn't like Kelly getting scratched today. I know it's just being paranoid, since zombies don't last very long in water. But you never know. Maybe the zombie germ does.

The truth is, nobody knows for sure how it happens. They don't even know what causes the disease in the first place.

Except maybe the government, and they're not talking.

"Why'd they move the Omegaman training facilities off LI?" I ask Kelly. "After the second flood, I mean."

"Well, the island was pretty much a lost cause," he answers, reciting history that both of us supposedly learned years back. I've since forgotten so much of it. The explanation sounds familiar, but it also sounds too convenient, like a lie. "The Army Corps of Engineers went in and walled it off and evacuated any people still alive."

That was the official account. Unofficially, I've heard there weren't any of them left.

"Grandpa says the Marines moved the Omegaman training facilities to Washington State seven or eight years ago. He says they were just going to let the remaining IUs keel over."

Most zombies just sort of run out of energy after a while, contrary to the old stories about them. Without human flesh, they'd last maybe a year. After a dozen years, the place would essentially be free of them.

About four or five years ago, Arc Properties went in and reclaimed some of the zones. They said they were going to do a survey. While they claimed to have found a few active zoms, the ones they did find were so slow that they were harmless. Of course, nobody cared a whit by then. Nobody wanted to go and re-inhabit the island.

Year before last, Arc Properties converted one of the zones into a new type of gaming arcade, which they called Gameland. They imported a whole new crop of fresh zombies as Players.

"Arc," Kelly spits. "Bastards." It's the only time I've ever heard him say anything bad about the company. It comes as such a surprise now because for the past couple of years, the rest of us talked about joining the company after high school and Kelly was actually pretty supportive of it, even though he had different plans.

"What, Kel?"

He shakes his head bitterly. "Rich bastards. All they care about is money. Did you know it costs a million bucks to buy into *The Game*? And that's not even for a good zombie, but an older one, probably with a first gen L.I.N.C."

I frown, wondering where this hostility is coming from and why he's all of a sudden talking about Arc and *The Game*.

"People who have that kind of money should use it for good instead of just throwing it away. If I were that rich, I'd make sure Kyle got treated."

I lean away from him.

His eyes clear. "Sorry, Jess. I guess I'm just a little tired after everything that's happened today."

He gets up and fetches his clothes from the dryer. "Think I'll head home."

Chapter Eight

Ashley pings me that evening. Thankfully, she waits until after dinner this time. Grandpa and Eric are at each other's throats again in the kitchen. At the moment, Eric's shouting and Grandpa's sitting there with his trademark military composure, which only seems to infuriate Eric all the more.

I close my bedroom door, muffling their voices.

"What's up?"

"Reggie wants us to meet at his place," Ashley says. "Can you come?"

"Right now? Um, I guess. What's this about?"

Stupid question, of course. There's only one thing it could be about.

"He's figured out how we can do it."

I snort. "Right."

"Just be there, okay?"

As soon as she disconnects, Kelly pings me. "You hear?"

"Just got off with Ash, but she didn't give any details, just told me to meet her at Reggie's."

"I guess they got equipment."

"What equipment? Scuba gear? How?"

I slip into my sweater and sneakers as Kelly explains.

"Apparently Ash knows this guy whose uncle owns a shop on the edge of town."

"A dive shop? Really? I don't remember any dive shops around here."

"Not so much a dive shop as a military surplus store."

I pause to think. "Are you talking about Eppy's over by the old hospital?"

"I guess. I stopped by Micah's on the way home. He said they were going to meet with this guy Ash knows. They invited me to go with them."

"Did you?"

"Reg was there."

I can tell by the way he says it that he still believes Reggie pushed him over the railing down in lower Manhattan.

"So?"

"Anyway, I had to get home and help out with Kyle. But Micah pinged me just over an hour ago and said they got everything we'd need, even wetsuits." He paused. "Apparently there's a catch, though."

"Yeah, money, that's the catch."

"Maybe. Micah didn't say, just told us to come to Reggie's tonight."

"Wait, you knew about this an hour ago and you didn't tell me?"

"Well . . . . I didn't want to ping you during dinner."

I grumble, but I know he's right. The last thing he'd want to do is interrupt my supper for a second day in a row, especially if he and the others hope to get me to come out afterward.

"Stop by and pick me up?" he asks.

"Yeah, give me about ten minutes. I think Grandpa and Eric are still arguing downstairs, so I'll try and sneak out. Otherwise, I'll have to think of something. I can't just say I'm going over to Reggie's."

"Tell them you're going to Ashley's then."

"That's like two miles away. Eric'll offer to drive. Then what?"

"You'll figure it out."

"I always do, don't I?"

Eric is still ranting in the kitchen, going off about some plan to expand the duties of his department at work. He's standing at the sink and flinging soapy water around as he washes the dishes, his back facing the doorway. "As if I don't have enough paperwork to do already!"

Grandpa's sitting in his chair leaning back. He's got his hands laced behind his head and he isn't moving. Just as I'm about to turn the corner, his chair turns and he looks at me. He doesn't say anything, just looks.

"I'm, uh . . . ." I point at the door. "I'm going over to Ash's. Me and Micah and Reggie and . . . Kelly. They're picking me up, so I don't need a ride."

He just sits there while I mess with the strap on my backpack. Finally he says, "Don't forget your medicine." Then he turns back around. Eric isn't even aware of what's happening behind him. He's still talking a mile a minute.

I slip out into the night and hurry over to Kelly's as fast as I can, afraid that if I turn around, I'll see my grandfather standing there watching me.

"That was quick," Kelly says.

"Yeah, well, things at my house are a bit explosive right now. Sounds like there's something going on down at the police station."

Kelly looks over. "Is everything all right?" He means did stealing a copy of Eric's inner zone permit cause any problems.

I shake my head and say, "It was something about having to do more work."

"Wonder if there's been another outbreak." He tilts his head like he's thinking.

I shrug. "I haven't heard anything about one."

My brother works in the Necrotics Crimes Division. Basically anything to do with offenses committed by or against the Undead is his responsibility. It's generally agreed that NCD is the suckiest job on the force, but it fits Eric's personality to a tee.

"Can we talk about something else?" I ask, and Kelly nods.

Ten minutes later we're standing on Reggie's front walk. We hear a low whistle and see Micah standing in the shadows beneath some tall bushes. He waves us over. "This way. We're in back."

"Why all the secrecy?"

"Reg's mom."

Kel and I both nod. Mrs. Casey is the nosiest woman on the face of the planet. If she got a whiff of what we were planning, she'd be on it like a bloodhound on the trail of a killer.

We circle around the house to the garage. Reggie's father had it converted years ago into a retro game room. There's a pinball machine and some ancient video arcade games, a pool table with worn felt and a ping pong table. It's totally lame, but the older generation seems to like it. That's why we hang out at Micah's instead, even though his basement is musty and the couch sags and smells like dogs and stinky feet and the downstairs bathroom should probably be condemned. Or at least fumigated.

"Hey guys," Reggie says, meeting us at the door. He's smiling. He hands me and Kel one of his father's beers and waves us in. I see that Micah's already got a bottle and that it's nearly empty. "I hope your weekend's clear, because we're shooting for Saturday. Whoever can make it, that is." He looks pointedly at Kel. "Right now there's four of us."

Kelly stops. "Four?" He looks over at me. I give him a quick shake of the head to indicate it doesn't include me. "Who's the extra?"

Reggie gestures with his beer behind us.

We turn just as someone says, "I am."

Stepping out from behind Ashley is a boy. I recognize him immediately. His name is out of my mouth before I realize it: "Jake?"

Kelly does a double take.

"The kid from this morning?" he says. "This is the guy who was hitting on you at karate?"

Jake raises his hands. "Whoa, wait a minute. I wasn't—"

"What are you doing here?" I exclaim.

"Wait," Kelly says. His face is starting to turn red. "Let him finish what he was going to say. I want to hear this."

I frown my displeasure, silently willing him to drop it.

"You two know each other?" Ashley asks, as she swings around Jacob to stand between him and Kelly. I can tell she's amused by this unexpected development.

"No, they don't," I say. "Not really. And I just met Jake this morning."

Ashley turns to him, raising her eyebrows. "You didn't tell me—"

"Jessie gave me really good a workout," Jake says, glaring back at Kelly.

Kelly takes a threatening step forward. I pull him back. "It was nothing," I say. "We sparred. At the dojang. There weren't any other students around so I—"

"No one else was around, Jess? You didn't tell me that."

"We weren't alone, Kel! Rupert was there." I turn to Ashley, eager to change the subject. "I don't understand, Ash. How did Jake get involved in our little . . . outing?"

"He knows about LI. Everything. And Jake was my lab partner last year, so . . . ."

I narrow my eyes. Ash always hated science. And yet I seem to remember she got an A in the class, though. "*Just* your lab partner?"

She shrugs and doesn't take the bait. "Look, guys, we needed equipment. I got it for us. That's all. There's no conspiracy, no *quid pro quo* here."

"Fancy words," Kelly grumbles.

"So your uncle owns Eppy's?" I say. "You're *that* Jacob Esposito? Little Jacob?"

Jake nods. "Nobody's called me 'Little' in a while."

"I remember you!" Kelly says. "Little punk on the playground, always picking on the smaller kids. What'd you, like, grow a foot over the summer?"

"Something like that."

Reggie comes over and manages to get between us all, somehow spreading us all apart to a safe distance. Kelly's still glaring, but the look in his eyes is not as hateful as it was a moment ago. Now it's filled with distrust.

"It actually works out having Jake join us," Reggie says. "He's a rescue diver and his uncle has all kinds of scuba gear. He's agreed to let us borrow it."

"Well, actually, it won't be scuba gear. And Uncle Joe doesn't know."

"In exchange for what?" I ask.

Jake looks around at the rest of us. "For inclusion in your little party, of course. I thought that was clear. I want to be included."

I narrow my eyes. "Why the hell would you want to break into Long Island? Don't you know it's illegal?"

"I do. And why would you?"

"Because we're hackers," I say. "Mostly anyway. Isn't that what you called us this morning? Jackers? That's what we do."

"Maybe. But hacking isn't the same as physically breaking into a Forbidden Zone." He shrugs. "That's where I can help. I've done all sorts of survival training. What can I say? I'm more of an outdoorsy type." He pauses. "Computers, on the other hand, well, that's just not my thing."

"And now there's an even number," Reggie says, giving Kelly a look.

"Why is that so important?" he asks.

"The first thing they drill into your brain in survival training is that you partner up," Jake answers. "You can do threes, but it's best to have twosomes, especially in a dive group. You both watch each other's back." He glances at me, and I don't know if it's just my impression, but that hungry, animal-like look is back in his eyes. I feel Kelly tense up next to me, even though we're not physically touching.

"And anyway," Micah quickly adds, "once we told him we needed the equipment, it's not like we could exclude him."

"You'd squeal on us?" I ask.

Jake pauses just long enough before shaking his head. There's little doubt what he'd do.

I sigh and throw my hands up in the air. "Fine."

"I'm not fine with it!" Kelly shouts. "I don't trust this guy as far as I could throw him."

"Don't go then," Jake counters. There's just a hint of a grin at the corners of his mouth.

"If Kelly doesn't go, then I don't go."

Jake's grin falters.

"Guys," Ashley says. "Don't be like that. Jake can partner up with Micah." She gives Micah a wink.

Suddenly I'm not thinking about Jake and Kelly, but Micah. This new question enters my mind. In the year or so that I've known him, have I ever seen him with a girl? I mean, other than just hanging out with me and Ash. Micah's always been the spare tire of our group, though it never felt like that big of a deal. There was never any jealousy at all.

Reggie raises his bottle for a toast. "Tomorrow, Jake's going to give us a quick lesson on diving using this special gear he's getting for us. Tonight, we plan. We need to figure out what to take. I'll look at the tide charts, all that stuff. Then, assuming the currents are right, we'll shoot for Saturday morning."

"Tides are on a roughly six-hour cycle," Jake adds, "so that'll give us a few hours to hang out before we need to come back." It bothers me how much he's inserted himself into the plan. And into our group. It doesn't feel right.

"Don't worry, Jess," Reggie says, misreading the concern on my face. "We'll have you back home long before dinnertime."

Micah and Ash clink bottles with him. I raise mine too, but don't drink. I notice that two other bottles are missing: Jake's and Kelly's.

I sigh unhappily, feeling as if my pent up excitement and worry are at war with each other. We're really going to do this. Or at least try.

But I'm not so sure I want to anymore.

Chapter Nine

"The oxygen rebreather was developed by NASA about a dozen years ago," Jake explains, holding the odd-looking mask up so that we can all see it, "and further adapted by the Navy for short-term underwater use."

It's just after eight o'clock in the morning and we're at the Page Mill levee and, except for some fishermen a few hundred yards away, we're all alone. The fishermen don't even bother to glance over at us. They look like they're well into their second case of cheap beer, and by the sounds of their singing, it doesn't appear they really care if they catch anything.

"Where's the air tank?" Ashley asks.

It's such a stupid question that I just know it has to be a set up.

Jake smiles. "I'm glad you asked that, Ash. By the way, I hope you don't mind my saying, but you look really . . . nice today." He turns to me and adds, "You both do."

Kelly makes a sound of disgust and looks away. Ashley beams. Of course she looks nice, she's wearing a skimpy white Ronnie Marx two-piece bikini that really highlights her red hair and green eyes. Not that any of the guys are looking at her hair or eyes. They're checking out the other assets that suit is also highlighting.

I look down at my own outfit, a pair of dingy oversized gray workout sweats. Underneath, I've got on a relatively modest rainbow-colored two-piece with French-cut shorts. Suddenly I feel like a shapeless blob.

"Thank you, Jake," Ash says, tossing her hair.

"What a loser," Kelly murmurs, too quiet for anyone else to hear, and for once I have to agree.

"As I was saying, the rebreather was developed to take the place of an oxygen tank, but primarily for use in short-term situations and tight spaces, such as between airlocks and docked vehicles."

"Are we traveling through any airlocks?"

Jake's eyes narrow. "You could say the tunnel is one long airlock."

"Just not in outer space."

"No." He clears his throat and continues. "The cartridge is perforated to allow pressure equalization. It's essentially a cage protecting an inner Mylar sack that contains a catalytic converter — beads linked to a chemical that converts cee-oh-two back into good old fashioned oh-two."

"Ah, good old fashioned oxygen. It's so much better than the new fangled stuff."

I snort and hip check Kelly. "Just ignore him, Jake. Go on."

"The rebreather wasn't intended for underwater use, but the Navy has been employing them successfully for strategic missions, rapid insertions and near-surface operations in confined spaces. They're a lot less bulky. Inert gasses, such as nitrogen are simply passed through the matrix, maintaining a proper balance and concentration relative to oxygen. That way your brain doesn't think it's either oxygen-deprived or in surplus. And that's important because either of those scenarios will cause you to faint. I probably don't need to tell you what happens if you faint while under water."

"Maybe you should explain it anyways," Kelly shouts. "You know, just in case Ashley hasn't figured it out."

I slap his arm and tell him to behave. Ashley gives him a dirty look and Reggie chuckles. Micah just sits and stares at Jake, whose confidence has all but vanished.

He disengages a canister from the hose attached to the mask and holds it up. It's about the size of a tub of Cheezy Cheeze. "There's enough chemical converter in one of these to last roughly three hours, give or take. Ample time for us to get through the tunnel and out the other side. But, just in case, each of us will carry a spare on our belt. They're sealed. All you have to do is insert into the hose and twist."

Just in case of what? I think. I don't want to be underwater for more than hour. Then I wonder: How long does it take to swim a mile?

"Why not just use scuba tanks?" I ask.

"You have to be certified to get the tanks," Jake answers. "And it's illegal to rent them out to uncertified divers."

"Isn't what we're doing already illegal?"

"Look, guys," Micah says, inserting himself in front of Kelly, "it's either the rebreathers or we don't go. Jake's uncle would definitely notice six dive tanks missing. But these?" He holds one up. "They're cheap and disposable. They've got cases of them in the store."

"What the hell for?"

"Military surplus," Jake says. "Uncle Joe bids on closed crates at auction. He gets whatever he gets. You'd be surprised what people will come into the store to buy."

"We'll also pack a third set in a waterproof pack for the return," Micah says, steering the discussion back to the trip.

"Talk about overkill," Kelly whispers.

"Better safe than sorry," Jake replies.

"Who put you in charge anyway?"

"Kelly! Stop it! Please."

"The rebreathers work just like the old fashioned masks. Bite down on the mouthpiece and inhale. You also exhale through the mouth, but instead of the waste gas bubbling into the water and going to the surface, it goes into the bag and gets recycled."

He tosses the rebreather into a box and comes up with a pair of goggles.

"Now, with scuba, to clear your goggles of leaks, you'd normally exhale through the nose. With these systems, you don't want to do that because... why? Anyone?"

"You'll lose your air?" Ashley quips.

"Exactly. The canisters don't create oxygen, just recycle it. Lose it and it's gone. So unless you have gills, I'd suggest you pay attention. These goggles are equipped with their own clearing mechanism."

He points to a silver cartridge inserted into the elastic headband. It's about the size of a large hotdog. "This is highly compressed air. Just push the button on the top ... here... which releases a puff, thus forcing any water out the bottom. You can get as many as twenty puffs, but then that's it, so make sure your goggles are a good fit. They should be tight and well sealed. Otherwise you'll be looking out through water goggles for the rest of the dive."

"Speaking of the water, are we actually going to get in it today?" Kelly asks. "Or are we just going to sit here and listen to you?"

Jake's ability to ignore Kelly reaches its limit. His face flushes and he fumbles the mask. He was so confident last night, so confrontational, that I almost don't recognize him now. It sort of worries me, because it makes me wonder if he's a little bipolar. There's enough emotional drama in our group without adding his baggage to it.

"I, um," he stutters, "was going to say it's time to get — uh, to put on the equipment." He quickly turns and picks up a box behind him. "There's another crate in my van with wetsuits, weight belts, and fins. Everyone gets a set. I took a guess on the sizes." He looks at Reggie and adds, "Although some might be a little tight."

Reggie grins and turns to Ash and says, "The tighter the better." She slaps his arm and sticks out her tongue. But then she thrusts out her chest at him and laughs.

"Let me know if you need any help getting it on."

"Let me know if you need help getting it off," Ash counters.

The rest of us are used to this, but Jake's face turns so red that I'm afraid he's going to spontaneously combust or something.

To distract himself, he launches into a lecture on fitting and prepping our goggles. The spitting part to keep them from fogging up amuses Reggie, of course. He makes a show of hocking a nasty loogie into the lenses, much to Ashley's disgust.

We don't get to use the rebreathers right away. Rather, Jake has us snorkel around a bit near the shore so we get used to being in wetsuits and flippers and being neutrally buoyant, which I seem to be having trouble with.

At first I have too much weight on my belt and keep sinking. I quickly grow tired from trying to keep myself at the surface. It's frustrating, especially since nobody seems to be noticing. Kelly's ignoring me as he paddles around twenty feet away, as if he can actually see anything in the murky depths below us now that we've stirred up all the mud. Finally I give up and waddle ashore to take some of the lead weights off.

"Here, let me help you," Jake says, startling me. I'd thought he was still in the water. He yanks my belt and it falls from my waist. Holding one end up, he threads a pair of one-pounders off. "You don't need as much weight because you've got so little body fat."

I know what he's thinking. Although I'm not flat-chested, I'm definitely not well-endowed, either. And he obviously hasn't seen my fat ass.

But pointing these things out to him isn't going to make things any better. We're already stressed enough.

He reapplies my belt, checks to make sure it's snug, then waves me back toward the water. "Just let yourself relax," he says confidently.

Without Kelly standing right there, his nervousness has vanished.

I look out over the surface of the lake to where the others are still paddling around and find Kelly's faded blue swim trunks and his lily-white legs. He hasn't even noticed I'm not there with him. So much for buddying up.

After the belt adjustment, staying at the surface turns out to be so much easier. Diving down to the bottom and coming back up for air takes very little effort, too. It's only ten or twelve feet down and, with the flippers, only three or four quick kicks before I'm there. Once I get to the bottom, I relax. My body just sort of sits there, swaying gently with the movement of the water, neither rising nor sinking. It's just as I imagined being weightless would be like.

After a brief break and a light snack, we try out the rebreathers. Ash immediately gets into trouble with hers, complaining that she keeps forgetting and exhaling out through her nose, which means she has to surface to get a fresh lungful of air. I can see it in everyone's eyes: What we're doing isn't just dangerous, it could be fatal if we don't pay attention.

After about the fourth or fifth time this happens, Micah lays into her. He tells her there won't be air pockets inside the tunnels. The frustration is written all over his face. He's worried about her, but I can see that he's only trying to scare her into remembering. "You need to remember not to exhale through your nose, Ash," he practically shouts, "or else you'll be in deep shit."

"I'll try," she says. Her lip quivers. I want to go over and protect her, but I know it's for her own good. She needs to try harder.

"No," Micah snaps. "Don't *try*. You *have* to remember. Do whatever you need to do to remember, even if that means sticking corks up your nose."

Ash glares at him and we all stop and wait for it, the inevitable outburst. I can tell she's close to breaking. If there's anything I know about her, it's that she hates appearing weak. That's why she's always got this tough-as-nails exterior. Inside, though, she's fragile.

But then she snorts and laughs. "Anyone got any ABC gum? You know, already been chewed? I can stick that up my nose." And the tension melts away.

After another twenty minutes, during which Ash stays completely submerged, Jake takes us to the other end of the levee. There are some ruins, giving us a chance to explore a little while practicing moving around and through obstacles.

"Make sure you always know where your partner is. The idea is to get used to swimming while watching out for each other. And remember, we're not here to become underwater salvage experts or anything. No wandering off."

He hands us each a waterproof flashlight and tells us to follow him. We all obey, grimly glancing around at each other, yet barely able to restrain our excitement. Even Kelly's eager to give it a go. There's a glint in his eyes that wasn't there earlier, despite his initial reluctance. I smile tentatively at him. He takes my hand and asks me if I'm having fun yet.

"I am now." And I give his hand a squeeze. We quickly kiss, then splash into the water. We're the last pair in.

The ruins are surreal, nothing like anything I've ever seen before! I mean, they're only an old two story commercial structure that happened to be built on a low point of land before the flood, but still. For the first time, I really begin to appreciate the old buildings and stuff we lost when the waters rose and covered the Wastes. Whole worlds of forgotten places where, just a single generation before us, people lived and worked and played. They slept in these buildings. They made love and they . . . .

They died.

My heart falters. I wonder if anyone died in here. Or drowned. I wonder if a person who had drowned would return. What would a zombie do after reanimating underwater?

We emerge from the one ruin and float over to the upper story windows of a second building. All of the glass has been broken out, most likely by the rising waters themselves, but maybe also by scavenger divers and thrill seekers. Nothing's left inside. All the old furniture and fixtures are gone, leaving just an empty shell, which is now caked with mud and lake debris and storm wash.

Jake guides us through the rooms. I feel like I'm in the belly of a sleeping beast. Then a big, black hole opens up before us, an elevator shaft, gaping like the beast's gullet. We crowd around him as he enters it.

He waits until we're all there, then he shines his light down and we hover over the darkness that fills the space below like heavy water. We all look at each other and wonder the same thing: What's down there? Jake's beam of light gets soaked up before it hits bottom. It looks like a bottomless pit. Anything could be hiding in it.

He signals, flips over, kicks and begins to descend. Almost as effortlessly, Micah does the same and follows. Then go Reggie and Ash, just as smoothly, and I think that Jake was right, this is a lot easier than I'd expected. Kelly tugs on my arm and we head down.

The shaft continues for what seems like forever. I can feel my ears popping from the pressure. Some of the others can feel it too, because they're puffing out their cheeks to clear our ears as Jake had shown us earlier. We rest for a moment until everyone's ready again. I notice that Kelly keeps drifting upward and kicking himself back down. I make a note to remind him to use more weight tomorrow. I don't want him to have to waste energy keeping himself down.

Suddenly, a thousand bubbles of air dance their way past me. I look down and see Ashley's panicked face. Her flashlight, now forgotten, drifts down into the inky darkness as her hands flutter near her mask. Now I can see her trying to suck air out of a canister that's mostly empty. Her eyes widen and she starts to kick herself up. She shoves Micah aside. But I can already guess that she'll never make it out in time. We're too far inside the building.

Jake shoots past us and grabs her leg. She kicks and kicks, but he doesn't let go. I feel Kelly brush past me, aiming for Jake, thinking he's trying to keep her from saving herself. But before he reaches him, Jake has yanked Ash's goggles off and is holding it below her face. His thumb pushes the blue clearing button and a rush of air surges out and envelops her head. I see her open her mouth. She stops struggling.

After a moment, Jake gestures upward and we begin to surface. I take one last look down into the depths, to where Ashley's flashlight has settled on the bottom of the shaft, its beam stabbing weakly into the unseen chambers. Then I follow.

"I can't do this," Ashley gasps, as soon as her head pops up out of the water. "I can't. I'm sorry."

Reggie swims over to her and grabs the front of her wetsuit and pulls her close to him. "You can," he says. "You're tougher than the rest of us put together, Ash. You're tougher than me. You can do this."

She looks around at us and we all dutifully nod. None of us wants her to back out now, least of all me. I don't want to be the only girl in the group. But I'm also worried, and not just for her. I don't think Reggie truly understands how difficult and risky this will be.

But to me it's clear. Our margin of error is thinner than the edge of a razor.

Chapter Ten

After returning from our practice dive, we laze around in Micah's basement. Micah's halfway through a bottle of his parent's scotch. Kelly's back to playing *Zpocalypto* and Reggie and Ashley have disappeared.

Jake's there, but he's sitting on a folding chair on the other side of the room, watching from the shadows. Kelly reamed him on the way back for not telling us we could use the air in the goggles in an emergency. Jake claimed he was going to, that he wanted to drill into our heads not to rely on it, but it's clear that Kelly doesn't believe him. "What else have you forgotten to tell us?"

"Nothing."

The tension is thick in the room, and I can tell Kelly's just waiting for another excuse to say we're all nuts for trying this. I'm relieved when Ash and Reg return and she grabs my arm and drags me upstairs to find something to eat.

I look for anything with protein, but all I can find is an open bag of stale peanuts. I take a handful and start munching on them. Meanwhile, Ash digs into a carton of mint chip ice cream.

"Want some, Jess?" she asks, holding it out so I can see how badly freezer burned it is. I shake my head and mumble something about keeping my girlish figure. Sugar and I don't play well together. A moment on the lips, as they say, forty minutes on the treadmill. With my metabolism, even three solid hours a week of high intensity hapkido training can't keep an ounce of chocolate from turning into a pound of butt-lard.

Ashley, on the other hand, seems to be able to subsist almost exclusively on a diet of sugar and caffeine. She never exercises, much to my amazement, and yet never seems to gain a pound. Granted, the girl isn't exactly skinny to begin with, but neither is she fat. Her five-foot-five, hundred and twenty pound curvy frame is one hundred percent energy. She burns more calories just breathing for five minutes than I do over an entire tourney weekend.

"Besides, it looks too much like zombie flesh," I tell her.

"Mmm, yum," Ash replies, and we both laugh, even though it's obvious why zombies happen to be on my mind. "You'd think Micah's parents would have more food around," she complains. "At least not expired food. Even the milk in here is old and chunky. What does Micah eat, anyway?"

"Duh. Take out," I say, pointing to the overflowing trashcan.

I've never met his parents. Micah says his father is constantly away on business and his mother is constantly out of the country visiting relatives in Texas or Arkansas. According to him, she's pretty useless.

I know all about useless mothers, have had plenty of experience with one myself, but it seems to me that Micah's really only half correct: If his mom is useless, then didn't that make his father just as bad? He's never around either.

I'd once privately mentioned this to Kelly, but he just changed the subject. Of course, he'd had his hand stuck up my shirt at the time, so I couldn't be sure his response actually counted for anything.

"Honestly," I said, as he struggled with my bra, "has anyone ever seen his parents?"

"Really, Jess?" he complained. "You really want to talk about Micah now?"

"Not him, his parents."

"They're real. Don't worry about it."

There's certainly enough evidence supporting their existence: the pictures hanging on the walls and sitting on shelves, the female hygiene products in the bathroom (yeah, I'm nosy, so just shoot me). Micah's an only child so they can't be anyone else's but his mother's. Plus, the packages addressed to them that I occasionally see sitting around on the counter.

Ashley gazes mournfully into the empty ice cream carton. "Think we should make a run to the grocery store?"

I shake my head. "It's almost dinnertime."

She shrugs, then sets the carton carefully down on top of the trash bin, being careful that it doesn't topple the unsteady heap. I'm tempted to go over and gather the top of the bag and take it outside, but I know Ash would just tease me about being so motherly.

She grabs my hand as we head back downstairs. "I'm nervous about tomorrow," she says. But before I can respond, we're back downstairs, and I can sense she doesn't want me to say anything about her confession. Still, I squeeze her hand to let her know that I understand and feel the same way.

The party breaks up shortly after that.

"Meet back here by seven tomorrow morning," Reggie tells us. "High tide peaks at four, so we'll have till about ten to take advantage of the outgoing current. That means we should be suited up and in the water by eight thirty. Nine, at the absolute latest."

Chapter Eleven

I don't sleep a wink all night, so I'm dragging when I finally get up at five thirty the next morning after checking the clock a dozen times over the space of about ten minutes. A cold shower doesn't even help. I don't feel rested at all. I just feel jumpy.

The house is quiet when I creep down the stairs. Eric's already gone to work, his lone breakfast bowl in the sink waiting for him to wash it after his shift at the police station.

Grandpa doesn't eat breakfast. I don't know if he ever did, now that I think about it. I can't ever remember him doing anything but going out to the back porch for a smoke, his extra large mug of coffee in his hand, steaming into the air. Rain or shine. It feels like such an old habit that it makes me wonder if he's always done that, even back when it would snow. It's been twenty years since Connecticut was cold enough to get any. I bet he did.

I learned long ago to just leave him be. He doesn't like company when he goes out to the railing. He just stands there looking out past our backyard and all the other backyards in the neighborhood. Looking south. He never talks about what he's thinking. He never shares his secrets.

What does he see?

I don't know.

But he's not downstairs yet, so I grab myself some cornflakes and juice and sit down at the table to do a quick check on the Media stream.

Then I raid the cabinets.

I look for anything that won't get ruined if it gets wet: granola bars hermetically sealed in plastic, a bunch of emergency waters in disposable bag containers, a couple oranges. I'm busy packing them into my backpack when I hear someone's throat clear.

"Mom?"

She stands at the entry to the kitchen looking miserable, like a hangover that just won't end, and I realize that pretty much sums things up with her — has pretty much summed them up for the past fifteen years. Her hair's a mess and her nightshirt is stained and worn and has holes in the collar. She smacks her lips unappealingly, then scratches the underside of her left breast.

A shadow shifts behind her and some guy appears and brushes into the kitchen. He slaps her ass and grunts. It's a different guy than the one she brought home yesterday afternoon.

Hey! I want to scream at him. He looks like the wife-beater type, but I could probably take him easily, knock him down a few rungs. "Never be the aggressor," Master Rupert's voice councils me. But my anger shouts even louder: *Don't treat my mother that way.*

She grunts, and I think, *Why do I even bother?* If she doesn't care about herself, why should I?

"What're you doing, honey?" she asks me. The man, thinking she's talking to him, mumbles something about beer.

I sigh. "Just getting some snacks for later." I stare daggers at the man's back, but they bounce harmlessly off. "I don't know if I'll have time to come home for lunch. In fact, I may be late for dinner."

She slips from the wall, tilting like gravity can't make up its mind today which way to pull. She seems to fall into the kitchen. For a split second I expect her to land splat on her face, and my heart almost stops. But she catches herself. She manages to limp to the table and sink into a chair.

Meanwhile, Mister Penis-du-jour is bent over in front of the fridge, probably confused by the milk jug sitting directly in front of the incomplete six pack of Hudson River Pilsner. Micah calls it Piss-ner and refuses to drink it. It's that bad.

"Did you hear me?" I ask. "I might not be home for dinner."

"Okay, honey."

I give her a chuff of disgust before I snatch my backpack from the chair and whirl out of the room. As I do, I hear the top of a beer can pop open. Then a second. The front door slams behind me as I flee.

Kelly sees me from his bedroom window before I turn up his front walk. He intercepts me with a whistle. I tilt my head up and blink against the bright sunlight reflecting off the glass.

"Be right down, J," he whisper-shouts.

I stand in the coolness of the porch overhang and wait. It's already warm. The temperature is supposed to peak at just under a hundred today, and humidity is high. Just another average August day in Greenwich, and the thought of slipping into that cool water actually takes the edge off the fear gnawing at my gut.

The door creaks open and Kelly slips out. He gently closes it behind him, acting as if the soft click of the latch is as loud as a gunshot. I give him a questioning look and he exhales through his pursed lips. He gives me a quick shake of the head. I notice dark circles under his eyes.

When we get to the sidewalk, I ask, "You couldn't sleep either?"

"It's Kyle," he says. "He's finally sleeping now, but he had another rough night last night."

I nod. Kyle's had a tough go of it. He had kidney failure when he was barely two and almost died. He managed to get a new one, but he's always sick. He often has these spells where he spikes a fever and screams as if he's in terrible pain. Nobody knows why. The only thing that makes it stop is exhaustion. But he's a light sleeper and even the slightest disruption can rouse him, starting it all over again.

I can see the strain of this most recent episode on Kelly's face.

"Are you sure you want to do this?" I ask. "I'll stay home with you instead of going. They don't need us."

He turns to me, but the look on his face isn't one of relief. Instead, he shakes his head and says. "No, I'm going." Then he adds, "Someone's got to pay the bills." I know what he's referring to, just not what he means. It's such a random thing that all I can do is simply dismiss it, chalking it up to his fatigue.

The financial strain on the Corbens has been almost unbearable for them. Kelly's dad works two jobs and his mom stays home to care for Kyle. Kelly has offered to start working a part time job — he's also hinted that maybe he should go work for ArcWare after graduating — but his parents are adamant about him going to college.

He hoists his backpack onto his shoulders and together we head over to Micah's.

"What'd you bring?" I ask.

"Lunch. Water. A few . . . other things."

I nod. "Me, too." But his pack looks much heavier than mine and I wonder what 'other things' means.

He sees me looking over. His eyes soften and he says, "It's a surprise."

"A picnic in zombieland? How romantic."

He laughs. "Not exactly."

Micah, Ash and Reggie are already waiting for us when we arrive, a few minutes after seven. I throw my pack into the trunk along with the rest of the gear: a couple other backpacks and a pair of large duffles.

" 'Bout time you guys showed up. Thought you were going to back out."

Reggie gives Kelly a long, meaningful glance, waiting for him to reply. But Kelly doesn't respond. He opens the back door of Micah's car and slides in. I notice he's still got his backpack tucked under his arms.

"Not much of a morning person, is he?"

I roll my eyes and tell him to cut Kel some slack, that Kyle had a rough night. Reggie's aware of the deets — they all do — and he immediately backs off. I'm glad. It just feels like so much of my effort is being spent on pretending everything's fine between everyone to have to pile the Corbens' situation on top of the mix.

I push in next to Kelly. He's got his Link out and is scrolling through it. I peek over his shoulder and see the ArcWare logo flash by.

"Go back," I say.

"What?"

"What was that?"

"Nothing. Just dumping a bunch of old messages."

"Are you applying for a job at ArcWare?"

"I said it was junk, Jessie."

"Can we go, folks?" Micah says, calling over to Reg. "We need to take advantage of the outgoing current. It'll switch directions around ten. I don't want to be fighting it."

Ash and Reg pile into the car. Once more I'm relegated to the middle of the back seat, but it's just a short drive out to the edge of town, so I don't mind. We're meeting Jake behind his uncle's store. From there, we'll head down to Manhattan.

When we arrive, Micah slowly drives around in back, where we see Jake's van with its door popped open. All the windows of the whitewashed building are barred and there's spotlights shining everywhere, even though the sun's up.

After he stops, we all tumble out but leave the car doors open, as if we're afraid of making any noise, setting off any alarms. Micah whistles and Jake slips out the heavily-screened metal door of the store. It bangs shut, making us all jump.

"Uncle Joe's at an auction up in Albany," he shouts down at us, grinning. "There's nobody here." He draws us around to the van and shows us the booty he's gotten for us. "We'll divvy it up when we get there."

Looking at the hodge-podge of equipment, I suddenly realize how little planning we've actually done for this trip. Other than the diving part, that is, and figuring out when to go and come back. And even that now seems pitifully inadequate. For such a dangerous proposition, you'd think we'd be better prepared. It's like we're all in denial. It's been such a surprise how easy everything has happened so far, relatively speaking, that nobody wants to tempt fate by questioning our good fortune.

But now I take the opportunity to bring up the possibility of encountering zombies. I know the others don't believe there'll be any, but still. "Shouldn't we bring weapons?" I ask. "You know . . . just in case."

Reggie wraps his arm around my shoulder and says, "You're a black belt, aren't you? Isn't that considered a lethal weapon?"

Kelly rolls his eyes, but I have to give him credit for not freaking out about Reggie's arm. It seems he can only be jealous of one guy at a time, and right now Jake gets the honors.

Jake holds up a bandolier and pulls a sick-looking knife out of a sheath. "We'll each get one of these." Then he pulls a couple of longer blades from one of the packs. "I've also got a couple machetes, if anyone wants one." He runs his thumb along the edge so we can see that they're not very sharp.

I shudder, and both Ashley and Kelly shuffle uneasily next to me.

Micah steps forward. "We won't need them. They're just going to be extra weight and get in the way. Besides, we'll only be there a few hours. Four tops. We get in, take some pics for proof that we were there, do a little exploring, pick up a couple small souvenirs and . . . ." He pauses and looks at each one of us. I can smell alcohol on his breath, but he appears to be perfectly sober. "Remember, we need to leave there by three o'clock at the absolute latest."

"The Colonel," I say, sighing. "Yeah, I know."

"Actually, I was going to say because of the currents."

"And the curfew," Kelly reminds us.

"Who's the Colonel?" Jake asks.

"My drill sergeant grandfather. He's got it in his mind that I have to be home every night for dinner. He runs the house like he's still a general and we're his Omegas."

Jake frowns in confusion. I wave it off. "It's a long story."

"Bottom line," Micah says, trying hard to get us back on track, "we're not there to take heads. Right, Reg?"

"Aw, why not?" he pouts. "I was all itching to kick some Undead booty!"

"There aren't any, remember?" Micah says. "But in the unlikely event that we do see any, I'm pretty sure they'll be so worn down and slow that you could sneeze on them and they'd fall over."

"Speaking of sneezing," Kelly says, turning to me, "did you remember to bring your inhaler?"

"You're as bad as Grandpa," I say, but when I pat my pockets I realize it's not there. I remember taking it out right after breakfast for the first of my three daily puffs, but then . . . .

Then Mom and her creepy new boyfriend happened. I must've left it on the counter.

I wince, waffle for a moment, then shake my head. "Can we make a quick detour at the house?" I ask.

Micah's face sours.

"I already missed two doses yesterday, plus this morning's."

He checks the time on his Link and grumbles. "We're already running late. Why do you even need that thing? I don't think I've ever seen you have an asthma attack."

"It's not for asthma," Kelly says. He sounds like he's had to explain this a thousand times.

"Then what the hell is it for?" Reggie asks. "Vitamins?"

"I just need it, all right?" I snap. "Please. It'll be quick."

Micah sighs. "I'll run Jessie and Kel over to her house. We'll catch up with the rest of you guys at the parking garage. You can start getting the equipment ready for everyone. If we leave now, we should only be about fifteen minutes behind you."

"How is Jake going to get through the checkpoints?"

Jake points to the back bumper. "It's got interstate tags for commerce. Uncle Joe uses the van when he does deliveries."

"Okay then," Reggie says. "Are we good?"

"I just need to lock up," Jake answers. He reaches for Kelly's backpack. "Want me to take that?"

Kelly swings it out of his reach. "I got it."

He doesn't notice the curious look Jake gives Reggie, but I do, and it makes me wonder once again why Kelly's being so defensive. But Micah tells us to hurry up and get in and even before I've got the back door closed, he's spraying gravel.

Looking back, I see Ash and Reg climb into the van while Jake heads up the steps to lock the shop.

Chapter Twelve

"**Finally!**" Reggie yells at us as we drive into the parking structure. His voice booms through it, sounding eerily hollow.

I had pinged the others to let them know we were going to be later than we'd expected because Grandpa decided to give us the fifth degree and the guards were hassling us.

Apparently the guards also hassled Jake. They'd torn the van apart, searching it. But they found nothing, and finally accepted his explanation that the equipment was for the store.

Kel and I tumble from the car. "Is it too late to go?"

Micah walks over from the rail. He shakes his head. "The tide's still going out. We should be okay."

"The direction of the current will change in about an hour," Jake says, checking his Link. "If we don't leave now, we'll be swimming against it."

This snaps us all to attention.

Ash comes over and hands us our wetsuits. "I've been watching for the cop," she says. "Same as the other day: there's just one on patrol." She looks at Reggie, who tilts his head at her and gives it a quick shake.

He says, "It looks like they're on the same sixty-minute schedule. He comes, hangs around for about ten minutes, then leaves. His last check was twenty six minutes ago, so ...." He checks his Link. "We've got about twenty minutes to get suited up, grab our gear and get under water before he returns."

"I still think that's odd," Kelly says. "Why patrol? And why with such regularity? They might as well announce to the world, 'If you want to do something illegal here, you got about thirty or forty minute window to do it in.' "

"Bureaucracy," I say. But something about it troubles me too.

Ashley opens her mouth to speak.

"Enough jibber-jabber," Reggie quickly says. "We need to hurry to make our window. Otherwise we'll have to wait till tomorrow."

Jake has already arranged the gear. Luckily, I've thought to wear my swimsuit under my sweats. The guys did too, but Ashley hesitates. Then she shrugs and strips off her shorts and tee shirt, right down to her undies.

Jake stares openmouthed until Reggie slaps him upside the head. "Give the girl some privacy."

Out of the corner of my eyes, I see Kelly smile.

I go over and block the boys' view.

"I can't believe you forgot your swimsuit, Ash." A part of me wants to believe it was an honest mistake, but I can't help wondering if she did it on purpose, like she's hoping she won't have to go. She pretends embarrassment, but then doesn't even try to be discrete.

"Well, you forgot your inhaler," she counters. I snap my mouth shut. Her actions haven't put the trip at risk. Mine have.

After the suits, we don our knife belts and hoist the waterproof backpacks onto our backs. Each one contains a pair of oxygen rebreather cartridges, light sticks, food and water and any other stuff we've brought. An extra cartridge is Velcroed onto our weight belt, along with a flashlight and another light stick. Each flashlight is attached to us on a short tether, so if we drop it, we won't lose it.

Kelly's off to one side, his back to us, transferring what he brought into the sack he's been assigned. I want to go over and see what he's brought, but I know he'll be upset if I do. He already told me once it's a surprise, and I don't want to ruin whatever it might be. Every once in a while, he gets a little romantic streak in him. Doing something special on LI would definitely give us something to remember.

Jake finishes getting geared up before the rest of us. He passes around our goggles and masks, attaching the cartridges as he goes. "Kelly?" he says, tapping him on the shoulder. Kelly spins around as he stands, his eyes flashing. "Number three, right?"

"I'm three," I say, reaching over for it.

After our practice dive yesterday, Micah put numbered tags on the masks and goggles so we won't have to readjust them. They're in order by our first names.

Jake stares at me for a second before slowly handing me the mask.

"Everything okay?"

"S-sure"

He drops Micah's and Reggie's equipment in their laps. They're busy discussing last minute details. They mumble thanks before resuming.

"No prob."

I glance over at Ashley, remembering how much of a fright she gave us toward the end of our dive. But she looks as cocky as usual, as confident and assured of herself as ever. Maybe it's the way the suit clings to her body and her awareness of the boys' hypersensitivity to it. I don't know, but if she has any of the self-doubt left over from yesterday, she's definitely not showing it now.

Micah packs the last few things in his sack. I notice the old tablet computer and a few other electrical gadgets. I don't bother to ask what he plans on doing with them as it seems pretty obvious. He wants to find an old terminal and see if he can hack directly into the iVZ infrastructure using one of the old nodes.

Whatever. I doubt we'll have enough time to find a working node, much less figure out a way turn it on, if it isn't already, *plus* physically splice into it.

He checks his Link and announces that we've got nine minutes at the most before the next patrol. It'll take us three of them to get down to the walkway, leaving us only six minutes of leeway.

"Ready?" he asks. "Last checks. Let's make sure everyone's good to go."

We buddy-check to make sure there aren't any loose belts or straps and that everything that needs to be sealed is sealed.

"Everyone got their Links?"

We all dutifully hold them up. They're strapped to our wrists so we won't accidentally drop them.

Micah holds his up and says, "Smile." Then we're all snapping photos of each other and laughing. Already I'm dripping with sweat and thirsty from the dry heat of the approaching day.

"Okay, enough of that. Let's go."

We shuffle off after Reggie, looking like a pack of upright seals that happened to get tangled up in a bunch of equipment. Kelly and I trail along in back. I look over and give him a smile. He smiles back, then turns his determined gaze forward again.

Then, before we know it, we're standing at the railing pulling on our flippers.

Nobody hesitates. We're all climbing over and are perched on the other side looking down into the water. None of us wants to think about what we're doing for even a second longer than we already have, because to do so would be to realize the insanity of our plan.

Micah takes a quick look around, then slides into the water, doing a perfect scissors kick that barely makes any noise or splash. We all follow, trying to imitate him.

A moment later, we pop back to the surface: six black lycrene-covered balls bobbing in the water. The coolness of it feels so good on my exposed skin. I was seriously starting to float inside my suit, standing out there in the heat. Everyone else looks just as relieved.

As one, we spit into our goggles, polish and rinse them, then slide them over our faces.

Micah signals to Jake, who slips his mask into his mouth, then his head sinks into the water.

Within seconds, the rest of us join him. The world and the hot sun and the noises of the dry August wind all disappear.

Visibility is about thirty feet. Light sticks begin to glow. A beam of light stabs the murkiness. Then, one by one, five more join it.

At nine thirteen a.m., we slide into the gaping mouth of the Queens Midtown Tunnel.

Part Two

Breaking In

We didn't so much break into Gameland as sneak in, although putting it that way might suggest it was a piece of cake. While it was easier than it should have been, there were more than a few problems, beginning almost as soon as we set off for LI. But each time trouble arose, we pushed even more doggedly on. I've lost count of how many times we should've turned around. At least a dozen. We should've cut our losses, but we didn't. Not once did any one of us even try to force the issue. We just kept right on going.
    Stupid.
    Of course, it wouldn't have mattered. Even before we slipped into that water, it was already too late to turn back.

Chapter Thirteen

Everything grows eerily quiet as the tunnel envelops us in inky blackness. The canned sounds of my own breathing and the ghostly inhales and exhales of my friends around me seem loud. Every once in a while, there's a *click* or a *tap* or some strange rattling noise. The sounds echo all around us, coming from everywhere and nowhere, telling us nothing about what might be making them.

    My eyes quickly adjust to the gloom. Five other glow sticks bob about me, looking like pastel St. Elmo's fires: yellow for Micah and Jake, green for Ash and Reg, and red for me and Kel. Six flashlight beams pierce the underwater twilight and illuminate a surprisingly open passageway.

    Several of the flashlight beams converge on a vertical divider, separating what was once the southbound and northbound tubes. Micah had mentioned this earlier, and by prior consensus we all kick to the right.

We've gone maybe a hundred yards in — it's hard to tell exactly how far since there's a definite push provided by the current — when my Link pings. I look down at the glowing screen and see it's Ash:

<< U OK? >>

I quickly type back while keeping an eye out for Kel's light next to me:

<< YES. U? >>

<< :o} >>

I type:

<< SO KUL >>

There's a pause and I glance up and try to identify which spot of green light up ahead is hers. Then, I get another ping.

<< :o] >>

I smile to myself and show the messages to Kelly. He nods and gives me a thumbs up, then urges me to catch up with the others.

We encounter our first obstacle about ten minutes later. It's actually not an obstacle, but it does make us stop. I don't see it at first. Kelly puts his hand on my arm and gestures ahead, shining his light.

It's a school of fish, small ones, thousands. Maybe millions. They move like a silver fog, and the water is so thick with them that it seems as if they're a single organism. We float there, entranced, until Micah waves at us and points to his Link, reminding us that we're running out of time.

The next obstacle, about twenty minutes later, nearly forces us to turn back.

It's a huge pile of garbage — boards, pipes, furniture, tree trunks, tires — all dammed up against the hulking carcass of an old bus. Everything's bleached to a universal gray-brown by layers of silt and mud and slime. The windows of the bus are opaque, hiding whatever might be inside. Seeing it, I wonder why there aren't more vehicles down here. I've seen all kinds of objects on the floor of the tunnel, but very few automobiles.

I get an urge to go down and inspect the bus — a sense of adventure, or maybe nervousness at not knowing what's inside — but once more Micah shakes his head. He points forward and I know he's right. We're not here to explore. Maybe if there's time on the way back we can. Of course, by then it won't matter so much. After LI, an old empty bus won't seem so new and exciting, even underwater.

Jake finds an opening against one wall, about half way up. It's roughly six feet wide and just as tall. The current is strong here, so we're careful as we wend our way through it, cautious of any sharp edges and loose objects that might cut us or fall on us.

The path through seems simple enough at first. Some sort of large metal frame appears to be both holding everything in place and preventing it from filling the opening. We grab it for handholds and actually have to "walk" our way through, since the current is quite strong.

Near the other end, we reach a mass of twisted wire and chain link fencing.

I look up just in time to see Reggie's hand slip. He crashes into Ash and together they slam into what looks at first glance like a solid wall. But their impact causes something to shift and pieces of garbage begin to rain downward. Something hits the cage above us, producing a loud *thong!*

We stop.

A large wooden dresser appears out of the darkness above. It tumbles down, heading straight for Ash. Reggie pulls her out of the way at the last second, and the dresser goes rolling lazily into the darkness below, where it lands with a muffled crash.

When the current washes away the mud and silt we've disturbed, I can see two yellow glows hanging in the darkness ahead. My Link pings. It's Ashley telling us she's okay.

Kel and I let go of our perch and slide through the end of the opening and out past the garbage dam. We time our kicks to avoid hitting anything else, twisting and turning past the unstable rubble. Micah and Jake are already ahead of us and closing in on the others.

Once the way ahead is clear, I send her a message back:

<< WAY 2 STAY KUL >>

I'd worried about her losing her air, but it seems that she's handling everything just fine.

She immediately pings back:

<< ABC GUM! >>

I almost laugh.

The screen suddenly blurs. I blink, but when that doesn't help, I try wiping my goggles, thinking they've fogged up. The blurriness remains. *The fog is on the inside of the lenses, stupid!* My head pounds. I'm starting to feel lightheaded.

I'm dimly aware of Kelly grabbing my elbow, but I can't move. He turns and gestures before coming back to me.

He holds up his Link for me to see:

<< OK? >>

I don't answer.

He shakes me.

Then Jake's there. I feel him yank on my belt. My throat hurts and my eyes are burning. Everything seems too bright.

A moment later, everything clears. The ache in my head is still there, but it's fading. My vision is clearing.

He shows me the used cartridge, then his Link:

<< FAULTY >>

Kelly shakes his head and glares as best as he can through his goggles and mask.

As we leave the pile behind, I wonder about that cartridge. Was it just an accident? Could it really be defective? How many of the others' are as well?

The garbage dam disappears into the darkness behind us. The tunnel ahead is wide and tall and, other than the occasional drifts of garbage along the floor and that one huge pile, it's remarkably uncluttered.

Micah — or maybe Jake, I can't tell which, just that it's someone with a yellow glow stick — shines their light on the sides of the tunnel. We drift pass old traffic signs and ancient graffiti, past the tendril remains of old wiring and pipes. Light fixtures dangle from the ceilings and walls, looking a little like the tropical moss that hangs from the trees along the south Connecticut coast.

A sudden burst of bubbles draws my attention to my right. We all hear it, stop and turn to look. It's Kelly and he appears to be struggling with his mask. In a panic, I swim over to him. His hands drop just as I reach his side. He frowns, waving me away. Then he points to his goggles. Relief washes over me as I realize he's just clearing them of water.

Our Links all ping at once:

<< EVERY1 OK? >>

It's Jake. We all give him a thumbs up. I can't really tell with the masks over our faces, but the look Jake shoots Kelly doesn't seem like concern as much as hostility. It's like there's this electric current running between them. But I still can't understand why Jake would harbor such feelings toward Kelly. Or is it just that he's sensing Kelly's jealousy? I don't know.

The look between them lingers a moment longer, then we're off again. I give a kick of my flippers and propel myself through the group. I want Kelly to catch up with me. I want to be in front for a while, instead of always in back and following.

Also, as long as I'm in front, I won't feel like I have to keep turning around and shining my light into the darkness, fearing that something is going to come out after us, a large fish or an alligator. Or shark. It's silly, I know, but I can't help it.

Even though there's this fear, it's not that bad. More like a shadow of fear, or a memory of it. There's obviously a sense of wariness and caution, just not the alarm I'd expect considering the risks we're taking. Maybe our excitement is neutralizing it. Or maybe it's the lack of sleep. I don't really care.

I keep kicking, feeling the strength in my legs. I know it'll be an effort for Kel to keep up, but I don't slow down. My Link pings. I ignore it.

I can feel my pulse beginning to pound inside my head. Out of the corner of my eye, I see a beam of light closing in, then the red glow of Kelly's chemical stick. He reaches out. His hand brushes mine, but I keep moving. That's when I sense the change in the water.

I slow. Then stop. Kelly slides up next to me. He holds his hands up, giving a wondering gesture. I look behind us and see that the group has spread out: two blue glow sticks between us and the two yellow ones further back.

I realize I'm drifting toward them. That's what Kelly's trying to tell me.

I raise my Link and quickly type:

<< TIDE RVRSING >>

I send it to everyone.

I can see the glow of five more Link screens, twinkling as they close the distance. A flurry of messages scroll across my screen, coming from Ash and Jake and Micah:

<< HOW FAR 2 GO? >>
<< WE'RE OK >>
<< NEED 2 HURRY >>

The others reach us, motion for us to stop for a moment. Micah types into his Link and sends it out to the group:

<< STLL TYM. OVR HLF WY. STY STDY >>

I can always tell when he sends a message because he hates using vowels.

He looks at me and gestures, as if knowing my thoughts. I nod, slowly and exaggeratingly: We need to push harder now or else struggle later. I thrust myself forward into the waiting darkness ahead. I can feel the others close behind.

I soon find myself pulling away from the group again. The sound of Kelly's breathing grows fainter behind me. I slow down to let him catch up, but it's Jake who reaches me first this time, Kelly close at his heels.

Kelly's breathing hard. The current is definitely strengthening, though it's not too bad. Yet.

I hear another rush of bubbles, and we all stop and wave our lights around until they find Reggie clearing his goggles. Ash and Kelly take the opportunity to clear theirs. I want to warn Kel to save his air, but I'd only be telling him something he already knows.

My mask is tight against my skin, sealed with Vaseline, as is everyone else's. A little water has leaked in, not much. I go ahead and raise my thumb and find the button just above the bridge of my nose and push.

Pressure on my eyeballs. My ears pop, then there's a sudden snap and my goggles slip away from my face. Everything around me suddenly goes blurry. I wave my hands around trying to find them, but I can't see anything. I drop the flashlight and its beam swings around before dropping to the end of its tether.

Air bubbles burst from my nose. Instinctively, I try to pull them back in and suddenly I'm coughing, choking. My lungs constrict. The air leaves my mouth, but not into the canister. It bubbles past my face and is quickly lost above me. Now my lungs are empty and so is my canister. I can't even find my goggles to use the compressed gas.

My ears are ringing, my throat constricts. I want to open my mouth and inhale and my mind screams at me, *No! No! Don't do it!*

I feel hands on me, on my arms and legs and head. Then my goggles are pushed into place against my face while another hand presses on the back of my head. There's an explosion of air and my vision clears. My lungs are beyond bursting.

The hand behind me forces my head down and another set of goggles is there. I'm not sure how many releases it takes before I realize there's air rushing up and into my face. I open my mouth and gasp, taking in putrid river water and air and I cough and gasp and cough some more and I feel like I'm drowning and going to die.

The air suddenly stops. Luckily, I've recovered my wits a little and my lungs are full. I feel my mask getting shoved into mouth, but I still can't see because of the hands holding the goggles into place, trying to fix the broken headband.

I reach up and try to push them away, but they stay. I bite down and exhale explosively into the canister, then inhale just as quickly. The air tastes stale in my mouth, but it takes the edge off, so I repeat the cycle again and again until the dizziness leaves my head.

Finally, the hands holding the goggles move aside enough so I can see the Link held up into my field of vision. I blink and the screen comes into focus:

<< UR MASK BROK >>

I nod. *No shit.*

The words scroll up and a second line of text appears:

<< OK NOW? >>

I nod again.

<< CANT FIX. TRY 2 HOLD URSELF >>

The text slides up.

<< OR GO W OUT >>

I reach up with both hands and push against the mask. I need them to see. The other hands fall away. Now I can look around me, though my own hands limit my peripheral vision. I see the concerned faces gathered in a circle around me, treading water. Without letting go of the goggles, I manage to hold a thumb up and everyone nods and reciprocates.

They pull away, all except Kelly, who lingers a moment longer. Despite how little of his face I can actually see, what isn't distorted by the goggles and mask, it's obvious he's worried. He holds up his Link so I can read it:

<< DONT DO THT AGN! >>

He leans forward and plants his lips on my cheek. The kiss is cold, but it sends a surge of warmth through me.

He slips beneath me and retrieves the flashlight on the end of its tether and flicks it off, knowing I can't hold it myself now, not without letting go of the mask.

Jake slides into view, gesturing that we need to go. I'm not sure how far we've slipped back in just the few minutes that have passed, but it puts us further away from our destination. Once again, I'm holding the others back.

Embarrassed, I let the others go ahead of me. I hold back a moment, wondering if we should turn around and head home. I won't be able to swim very fast with my hands like this. And dispensing with the goggles so I can doesn't seem like much of an option, either.

Kelly tugs me forward, his hand on my elbow. Despite what I've just gone through, he doesn't even ask if I want to go back. It pisses me off. But already the rest are moving on, and I know he has no choice but to follow.

Neither do I.

Chapter Fourteen

My arms ache. My back is stiff. My legs are burning. And still we swim on.

If not for Kelly's hand on my arm, I don't know how I'd make it, since I can barely steer with just my feet. Even with him guiding me, I feel like I'm fighting against some invisible force that wants to turn me around. I'm moving as much sideways as forward. I try to correct my trajectory by twisting my body, but it doesn't help much, just makes me all the more exhausted.

The yellow and blue glow sticks pull away from us, begin to fade in the distance and the murk. I kick harder. My breathing grows ragged. My body's not used to this particular kind of exercise.

I can hear Kelly beginning to strain, too. Then, without warning, he jerks me to the side. His hand slips off of me and I'm bathed in blackness as the beam from his flashlight winks out.

Kelly?

I twist, but all around me is nothing but black ink and midnight loneliness. I strain my eyes through the goggles. They leak. I push them hard against my face.

Kelly!

But then the beam from his flashlight flickers on. It's way off to one side. It swings around, jerks, then sinks down to the floor. I wonder if the tether somehow came unattached from his belt.

I spin around, kicking to get myself turned, and my flipper connects with something that feels like it has some give to it. I cringe, thinking I've just kicked my boyfriend in the face. But when I extend my legs, there's nothing there.

The light below me changes. I see the faint outline of a figure holding it. The beam swings up and stabs at me. I swing my feet around and once again I feel a momentary resistance behind me.

A bubble of air escapes from my mouth. Water squirts into my goggles.

Kelly?

The light catches me square in the eyes. But then I feel a firm hand on my leg. I realize one of the others has come back, and I relax and wait for whoever it is to come alongside me. Without my hands, without my flashlight, I feel helpless.

The grips tightens, begins squeezing. I grunt when it starts to become uncomfortable. A second hand grabs my other leg.

Kelly's flashlight jerks back and forth below me, coming closer. He's swimming back up. I reach behind me to push the person off — guessing that it's Reggie by his strength — but when I turn to look, it isn't Reg. It's nobody I recognize.

The man's hair floats wildly about his pale face, and his eyes are gaping black holes. His mouth yawns at me and his teeth are yellow and ragged. He pulls himself toward my body. A tongue lolls out. It takes my mind a moment to process that he isn't wearing a wetsuit or a mask or goggles. *That's not possible,* I think, before realizing I'm in the grip of one of the Undead.

Air slips from my mouth and nose. My body contracts. The movement draws the thing even closer to me. The grip has hardened. It feels like a vise. It burns my skin as I kick desperately at it.

One hand lets go, reaches forward. I kick and scream inside my throat, but the hand finds my upper calf. The second hand releases me and somehow manages to grab me just above my knee. I slap at them with the goggles and kick. The zombie leans in to bite me.

But the grip slips on the slick material of the wetsuit, and it slides down my legs. For a moment I think I'm free. But then the hands catch on my flippers. Icy cold fingers wrap around my bare skin and begin marching back up my legs. I can hear the monster's teeth clacking together as it extends it rotting neck and mouth toward me once again, desperate to feed.

Then, suddenly, the thing jerks to the side. The motion pulls me along with it. I see a flash of silver and the weight on one of my ankles falls away. The hand is still gripping me, but it's no longer attached to an arm. I kick wildly, sobbing. Slowly the grip weakens and eventually the hand falls off. The blood seeping from it is thick and oily, staining the water black.

But this only seems to make the zombie angrier. It bats its oozing, jagged stump at me and begins to pull again. There's another thump from the side, another flash of silver, and I see Kelly's knife embeds itself deep into the zombie's neck. He wrenches it free and the wound tears open, revealing a tangled mass of atrophied muscle and veins and the thick cord of the monster's blackened gullet before the water clouds up with its gore. But still it doesn't stop coming.

By now I'm flailing my entire body in a panic. The goggles are gone. I'm kicking and it's not making any difference. I barely manage to remember to bite down and breathe through my mouth into the cartridge. It feels empty.

I remember the knife in my belt. I reach down and pull on the handle, but it won't come free! More air leaks from my mouth. The monster's stump hammers at my flipper.

No! No, no no nononono!

Somehow, my fingers find the snap holding the blade. They flick it open. I pull the knife free and try to bend over. Now the zombie is behind me, just out of reach. I twist desperately and hack blindly at the space near my foot.

More air escapes out of me. I'm feeling it in my lungs now, the lack of air. I'm feeling it in my throat. I'm feeling it behind my eyes and in my head and it screams for me to breathe, to open my mouth and take in a huge breath of air.

Blackness pushes against the edges of my vision.

The knife! Use the knife!

A pinprick of light forms in front of me. Grows. It's warm and whispering comforting things at me: *Breathe now, it'll be all right.*

I'm dimly aware that I'm still hacking, but my movements feel weak and pitiful. The blade connects with something rigid, jarring my arm, rousing me momentarily.

The monster twists and clacks. The knife is nearly wrenched from my hand. I feel the grip on my ankle loosen for a fraction of a moment before tightening again. *I've hurt it!*

I yank the knife free and hack again. There's more resistance, then the weight drops away.

I let the knife go and kick to get away from the body of the monster I can't see, the remaining hand still attached. Blinded by darkness and oxygen deprivation, my eyes burning from the filthy water, I reach down to pull it away.

The fingers are like plastic bands. I pry desperately at them. My stomach revolts, but to be sick now would be fatal. I finally manage to loosen the hand just as a bright light begins to fill my vision. *Kelly*, my mind prays, but deep down I know it's not him. The whiteness is in the space behind my eyes. It's my brain shutting down. The whispers grow loud inside my head.

I feel something caress my face. I open my mouth and water flows in. I cough, sputter, and open it again. I inhale just as another balloon of air envelops me. Kelly forces the mask into my mouth and holds it there, pinching my nose, willing me to breathe into my canister.

After a few minutes, I open my eyes. He holds me like that for several more minutes, until the black light inside me and the whispers fade away.

When I'm ready, he points the beam of his flashlight down into the darkness below us. I can't see much without the goggles. I don't know if he's showing me the zombie; I kick to get away, but he holds me until I stop struggling.

Once more he points the light down, then at his face, then at me. He means that we need to go down and find my goggles.

Still shaking from the encounter, still weak from lack of oxygen, I try to follow. He goes slowly, waiting for me.

When we reach the floor, he begins to search, sweeping his light back and forth. The floor is littered with objects washed in over the years. It all just looks blurry and shapeless to me.

I begin to think it's hopeless when his light reflects off something shiny. Kel dives down and comes up with my knife. He pushes it back into my sheath. Then he goes back down.

After a few more minutes of searching, he returns, shaking his head. He points to his own goggles, offering them to me. I tell him no and gesture that we need to go. We're completely alone. There's no sign of the other four. They haven't even noticed we're not with them anymore.

Kel grabs my hand and together we rise toward the ceiling. If the current wasn't pushing at us, forcing us back toward Manhattan, it'd be easy to mistake which direction we need to go. We angle toward the nearer end of the tunnel, not sure if maybe we aren't making a mistake anyway.

Within minutes, a point of light appears in the darkness ahead. It swings around like a strobe and grows quickly stronger until it fills the tunnel. I shield my eyes. A second beam joins the first. We swim hard for them. Finally, I see two yellow glow sticks dangling just below the light beams. Micah and Jake pull up beside us, gesturing frantically. Micah holds up his Link.

I reach down and pull mine up to my face, holding it close to my eyes to read. There's an old message there from Micah and it reads:

<< WHR R U? >>

I delete it and a second message pops up from a minute or so later:

<< ANSR PLZ! >>

Micah quickly types in a new message:

<< FASTR! >>

Anger fills me. There's no wondering whether we're okay. No asking what held us up. No apology for leaving us behind. I was attacked by a fucking zombie! I could have been bitten!

Excitement flashes in his eyes. He jabs his thumbs once more at his screen. My Link receives his post:

<< NRLY THR >>

I want to cry. I want to scream and kick and hurt someone, but I'm suddenly exhausted. Numbness overwhelms me. Kelly gently prods me forward and I follow. I can feel myself drifting into shock.

Sometime later — seconds? hours? I have no idea — I sense the blackness of the tunnel begin to weaken. I start to see the faintest details: seams in the walls, objects lying on the floor below. Even without goggles and a light I can see. We've reached the end of the tunnel. It begins to arch upwards and light breaks over us in ever stronger waves. We've done it. We've officially broken into LI.

And yet I'm too shaken to celebrate.

A moment later, we pop up out of the water. At a minute before eleven in the morning I get my first glimpse of a city that was abandoned to the Undead.

Chapter Fifteen

Reg and Ash join our floating circle. Everyone's speaking all at once, asking questions, laughing, yammering, demanding where the hell we were and what took us so long. They don't realize anything terrifying happened down there.

Jake notices my missing goggles and asks about them. He seems more worried about them than he is about me, but that may just be me being oversensitive.

Neither Kelly nor I answer any of their questions. Kelly brusquely waves them off, growling that we need to get me to land. I'm grateful for his strength. I'm grateful that I don't have to say anything or even think. I wouldn't be able to string two coherent thoughts together, must less words.

My shaking has grown much worse, as if my body knows that safety is within reach.

Or knowing that I'll have to face that horrible experience aging on our way back. I don't know if I'll be able to do it. Or how.

I'm faintly aware of Micah talking. He's telling us that the overpass where we've surfaced is too high to climb. It rises six feet over our heads. The wall extends to both sides, stretching about a hundred and fifty feet before turning back toward us. We spin around. The water reaches into the distance, fanning out wider and wider as it reaches the horizon.

Reggie points to a place where the chain-link fence has been pushed from its poles and now dangles into the water. It's only thirty feet away.

"We can climb that," he says.

He sounds as tired as I feel, and now I can see the fatigue on everyone else's face, the strain. And maybe a little disappointment, too. I don't know what they were all expecting — I know what I was before my underwater encounter: Pristine buildings, a preserved city. But all I see here is bleached out structures that look run down and dirty. The place is a ghost town. But, thankfully, it appears to be just as abandoned as Reggie had claimed it would be.

Or maybe that's why they're disappointed.

Kelly pulls me toward the fence. I let him. I can't seem to find the strength to move, so I just drift. Where does he find the energy? I look over at him and notice that he's straining his neck above the surface. He's scanning for any signs of trouble on land.

Despite having to tow me, Kelly's the first to reach the fence. He makes sure I'm holding onto it before he peels off his flippers and tosses them over. Then he climbs up. The fence sways and clangs, sounding too loud in the eerie quiet.

"Looks clear," he says, after a quick but thorough look around. The rest of the group begin to clamber up. Kelly reaches down and helps me. My arms are shaking so badly that I can barely hold on. I still have my flippers on. He practically has to drag me up.

I immediately sink to the ground. Everyone else is peeling off their equipment and unzipping the tops of their wetsuits. The sun is baking us, but I'm shivering.

Kelly doesn't bother with his equipment. He finds an abandoned car on the tunnel overpass and climbs up onto its roof. It's covered in dust and rust and tufts of grass. It creaks and rattles. He cups his hands around his eyes and scans the horizon. Reggie is the first to notice his odd behavior. He chuckles.

"Check out the brah! Already looking for IUs. I told you before there won't be any."

Kelly's eyes flash and he jumps off the car and rushes over. He slams Reggie in the chest and screams, "No zombies? Then what the fuck was that down there?" He points at the tunnel and everyone looks, confusion clouding their faces.

"Where?"

"In the goddamn tunnel, asshole! Where the hell were you?" Kelly turns to each of the others, glaring. "We were attacked by one down there! Jessie could've been . . . ."

His eyes suddenly grow wide and he rushes over to me. "Were you bitten?"

I shake my head.

The others are watching all of this in shocked silence. Then Ashley leaps to her feet and points at Jake and Reggie. "I told you guys we should've told them!"

Kelly's eyes narrow. "Told us what?"

Reggie sweeps over and stands between them. "We didn't know, Ash! How could we have known it was a zombie? It was too far away. We still don't know!"

Ashley ignores him. She peers around Reggie to speak directly to Kelly. "We saw one. And don't tell me it wasn't a zom either, Reg, because I know what I saw! Back there. Damn it, I knew it was a zombie, but you said it was just some homeless guy who fell in the water!" She hits Reggie on the chest.

My head snaps up. "What?" My throat hurts and my voice croaks. "You saw a zombie and you didn't think to warn us? You didn't ask, *Where the hell are Kelly and Jessie? Maybe they're in deep shit?* You just left us back there!" My voice has risen to a screech. I'm nearly in tears by now. "What the hell were you thinking? I almost got bitten! I almost fucking drowned!"

Nobody says anything for a moment, then Jake says, "It wasn't in the tunnel."

As if *that* excuses why they left us behind.

Kelly whirls on him. He's shaking with rage and sputtering almost incoherently. Finally a single word explodes from his lips. The f-bomb shatters into a million pieces across the city. In the distance, a flock of pigeons lifts off the ground before settling back down again a moment later.

Jake is clearly shaking. "It was while we were waiting for you in the garage. When Micah took you back to get Jessie's medicine."

"What the hell are you talking about?" Kelly screams.

"Keep it down, guys," I say. But the words somehow dry up in my mouth and flutter away like dust.

"I told you," Ashley cries. She hurries over to where I'm kneeling on the hot asphalt. "I told you we should have told them what we saw." She points at Jake again, thrusting an accusing finger at him. "But you just kept agreeing with Reggie. Why the hell would they call in NCD for a homeless guy?"

NCD?

"They called in Necrotics?" I stammer. "Was it Eric?"

Jake backs away. Reggie glares around himself looking like he wants to punch someone. Then he suddenly bends and picks up a chunk of rock and heaves it far out over the water. The splash sounds clunky and doesn't even echo. "We didn't know for sure what we saw," he mutters. "And, no, Jess, your brother wasn't there. At least, we didn't see him."

"Now we know why the cops patrol down there by the tunnel opening," Kelly says. "They're checking for swimmers."

Reggie shakes his head. "No! You said it yourself, Kel. If they were so concerned about breaches, why wouldn't they just block the opening?"

Nobody speaks. It's a valid question, one we've all been wondering for days now. Why make it so easy for zombies to get through? For that matter, why make it easy for people, too?

"It wasn't a zom," Reggie concludes. "It couldn't have been."

"Then why call NCD?"

"Swimmers?" I ask, shaking my head. Logically, I know zombies can't swim. In the water they're just as helpless as logs, drifting with the currents. But the one that grabbed me sure felt like it had taken lessons.

Kelly waves his arms helplessly. "Well, what else are we going to call them?"

"Floaters," Ashley says.

"The one that attacked us wasn't floating. It was like it was waiting for us."

"It wasn't waiting for us, Jess," Kelly says, but even I can see the doubt in his eyes. "It just happened to be there, I think."

I swing my head to Ashley. My neck feels stiff and creaky. "You actually saw them pull one out? Before we left?"

"What we saw," Reggie quickly answers for her, "was a cop dragging a body out of the water. A *dead* body. It wasn't moving, so, no, I seriously doubt it was a zombie. Besides, even if it was a zombie, it was dead. Don't you get it? It was totally dead. We had no way of knowing there'd be more in there. *Live* ones."

"He used a hooked pole and dragged it out onto the walkway," Ashley mumbles. "We watched as he pinged someone on his Link. A couple minutes later, NCD came in a van and carted it away."

"They didn't even use gloves!" Jake insists.

"What the hell does that prove?" Kelly snaps. "That doesn't mean it wasn't a zombie!" He grabs Jake's tee shirt and pulls them together until their faces are inches from each other. My mind screams at Kelly to be careful, but all I can do is moan. Jake doesn't fight back. "Everyone knows it takes more than skin to skin contact to pass the infection! It takes a bite. Of course he didn't wear gloves!"

"But, water— " Jake begins to argue.

"Bullshit!" Kelly's eyes shift over to me. Everyone's looking at me now, wondering if I swallowed any water down there. They have to be thinking I might've been infected. "Wearing gloves doesn't mean shit, you idiot!"

Ash hugs me closer. "Don't worry," she whispers into my hair. "G-ma Junie was wrong about that. Water can't transmit the infection."

I know she's just trying to cheer me up, to help me get past the attack in the tunnel, but it doesn't help.

I push her away and lean over to one side. The remains of my breakfast cornflakes and all the river water I swallowed come pouring out of me. Ash jumps back, not wanting to get splashed. The others watch in horror, afraid to get too close to me.

When I'm done, I feel a lot better. I get weakly to my feet and say, "We're wasting time. It must've been a fluke. There aren't any more zombies here, obviously, so let's do what we came for and get the hell back home."

I've lost all my enthusiasm for this game. I'm not having fun anymore.

The rest glare at each other for several more seconds before finally nodding. They busy themselves finishing stripping off their gear and stowing it. Ash and I leave our wetsuits on, keeping them unzipped to the waist.

While they're distracted, I pull my inhaler out of my pack. I take a long, deep hit. Then a second.

Just to be sure.

And I pray to God that G-ma Junie was right about the disease not being spread by water.

Chapter Sixteen

Reggie decides that we should all stash our diving equipment inside the trunk of the abandoned car Kelly had climbed on earlier.

"But keep your knives with you," he recommends. So we strip away the rest of the gear from the bandoliers and rebuckle them on our waists.

He opens the front door and reaches in and pops the latch. We all lean away, as if expecting something to come crawling out at us. But the trunk is empty, save for a spare tire, a single men's shoe — size nine and a half — and an umbrella. He tosses in his pack, mask and goggles. We each follow suit.

Micah's off to one side, messing with his Link and mumbling to himself. Reggie goes over to get his gear, but Micah waves him off. "Give me a sec."

"Ooh," Ashley says. She reaches into the trunk and pulls out the umbrella. She has to struggle a bit to open it up, and when she does, the fabric is so dry and flimsy that it immediately begins to disintegrate. Black flakes rain down on her head. What's left of it looks like a month-old sun-baked carcass: just the ribs and a few flaps of skin-like fabric barely hanging on.

Her silliness makes me laugh, and my laughter signals to everyone that it's okay to relax. I lean over and whisper in her ear that I'm glad she came.

"What should we do first?" Reggie asks, pouncing on the uptick in our moods.

Kelly glances over at me. His face is still filled with concern.

"I'm fine," I say. "Really. I'm actually up for a little distraction." I pause and add, "Just, a little, though. And promise me no more zombies. If I never see another one as long as I live, I think I'll die a happy woman."

"But then you'll have to be one," Jake says with all seriousness.

Everyone gives him a dirty look and his face flushes deep red.

"Are you always this clueless?" Kelly asks.

"Uh, guys?"

We all look up. Micah's off about fifty feet away, standing and staring off into the distance. He slowly turns to us, then raises his hand and points.

We all get up and walk over.

About a quarter of a mile away is a solitary figure. It doesn't move.

"Is that what I think it is?"

We strain our eyes, but it's too far away to tell. "Looks like a tree," Reggie says. "Or a statue."

"Or maybe it's a homeless guy," I say.

Jake reaches into his pack and withdraws a pair of binoculars. He trains it on the figure and adjusts it.

"Sorry, Jess. It's a zom. Naked. It's skin . . . ." He shivers. "Now I know what standing outside in the sun every day for thirteen years will do to you."

"Is it . . . dead?" Ashley asks.

"It's not moving."

He scans with the binoculars all around us before announcing there aren't any more.

"We'll just keep an eye on it, then," Micah decides. He comes over to me and asks if I'm okay. I nod.

"I don't know about the rest of you," Ashley says, "but I'm starving. I think we should eat."

"Beef jerky?" Reggie jokes. Everyone groans. But then he pulls a Slim Jim from his pack and laughs. "I was sort of hoping we'd see one just so I could do this."

"You really are a disgusting pig."

I grimace and clutch my stomach. It's still a bit touchy. "Not for me."

Kelly pulls out a Red Bull and opens it for me. "At least drink something then."

"It's warm."

"Drink."

I notice that nobody teases him for mothering me.

When we're done eating and resting and Jake has confirmed that the zombie hasn't moved in the last twenty minutes, Ashley jumps up and exclaims, "Pictures! We need pictures."

She whips out her Link and hands it over to Micah, ignoring Jake's outstretched hand. Jake gets this embarrassed look on his face and pretends he was reaching for something else. I can't help but feel a little twinge of guilt for him. He's trying so hard, but he's so obviously not figured out how to be a part of the group. I doubt he ever will.

Ashley plucks the umbrella from where she dropped it and starts parading around with it over her shoulder. She twirls it and says, "I feel like one of those flappers from a hundred years ago."

"More like a hundred and twenty years ago," Kelly says.

"Dude, do you have to be so freaking — I don't know — *literal* all the time?" Reggie says, then quickly adds, "Just messing with you, brah. Chillax."

Micah snaps a couple pictures of everyone in various poses, including a few zombie poses that strike me as both amusing and vaguely unsettling. Then he announces that he's got things to do.

"You guys go ahead. I'm going to try a few quick computery things. He pulls the old tablet from his pack, and a tangle of wires trails out.

"Still think you can hack into iVZ?" Ashley says.

Micah shrugs. He presses a button on the side to boot it up. "It's worth a try."

I frown. "Why? It's already coming on noon. We've only got a couple hours or so before we should get ready to leave."

"Um . . . because." He looks around us, as if it's obvious why. "We couldn't get into *The Game* before, but now that we're inside the ArcTech firewall . . . ." He shrugs and points to a spire in the distance. It's one of many that rise from the top of the wall every quarter mile or so. They're supposed to prevent implanted zombies from breaching the perimeter by frying their L.I.N.C.s if they cross it. It's also there to keep hackers from breaking in. Hackers like us.

Because of the intervening buildings, we can't actually see the wall at the moment, but we can see the EM towers poking up above the buildings. The air around them glimmers, almost as if we're looking through water. I know it's just an illusion, but it sure seems real.

Micah taps a few things on the screen and holds it up for us to see. It shows a map of where we're at and a cluster of tiny red dots. He zooms in and the dots assume labels. We all gasp.

"Hey, that's us!"

"You hacked our implants?" Ashley cries. Her hand instinctively reaches behind her head, as if she could block whatever connection Micah has made to it.

He shakes his head. "Actually, not directly. It was easy to hack your Links, and from them get your L.I.N.C. numbers. Once I had those, I coded in our implants into this old tracking app and embedded it within a geolocator." He points to the tower again. "The signals ping off the towers within range and triangulate back to me."

"Subtitles, please?" Jake says, looking bewildered.

"It means he can track wherever we go," Kelly says.

"W-why?"

"Wait a minute," I say. "Does that mean *anyone* can track us? At any given moment?"

Micah frowns at me. "Like the government isn't tracking each and every one of us already?"

"So, they know we're here?"

Micah shakes his head. "No one outside the wall can track us in here. The EM masks our signal, preventing anyone on the outside from seeing anyone inside. That's why nobody can hack the Players' implants. The only way to connect with them is through ArcWare's iVZ codices, which are tuned specifically to their nodes." He points to the EM spires. "And I'd be willing to bet you there's a node in each and every one of those towers."

Jake's still looking totally lost, but the direct implication of Micah's hacking is easy for the rest of us to calculate: another chance to access *The Game* and actually play it.

"It's simple, brah," Reggie patiently explains. "If you break the iVZ programming language, you can read *The Game*. But you still need to be able to connect to the Players. That's what the tracker does. That's basically what the ArcWare codex does. It's just a device. Anyone could build one, but without being able to speak its language, it would be useless. ArcWare uses a proprietary coding format written in interweaving layers, but now that we're inside, the entire language architecture is completely exposed."

"Meaning?"

"Meaning after we return," Reggie exclaims, "we'll be able to build a descrambling device and play *The Game*!"

Micah holds up his hand. "I still need to see if I can actually find and track Player signals. That's why I needed to hack your L.I.N.C.s. First, to prove the concept, then so I can subtract them out as background."

"I don't care about *The Game*," Jake declares. "And I don't want you tracking me!"

Micah chuckles. "I'll wipe all your numbers after we get back. Don't worry. It's only temporary."

Reggie slaps him on the back and says, "What are you doing standing around for, then? Get moving!" He rubs his hands together. "I can't wait to get back and wreak some havoc on some real zoms. No more *Zpocalypto* for this guy."

Ash's face lights up too, at the prospects. Even Kelly looks a bit more excited than a moment ago.

But something bothers me. If Micah is able to hack and track the Players' implants, then obviously the next step is learning how to control them. That's essentially the point of all this. So, if he's able to do that, what's to stop him from doing the same to us? Other than his promise not to, I mean.

I try to dismiss the thought. He said he'd get rid of our implant numbers. Besides, if it were even possible, then surely someone would've tried it already. As much as I distrust the government, they wouldn't allow something like that to happen, would they? Our implants are supposed to be inactive until we die. That's what the *latent* part of their name means.

Nevertheless, I keep my thoughts to myself. I don't want anyone else thinking it, or worrying over it. Or getting any ideas. Micah's not the only one of us with the skills to accomplish such a thing.

I turn around to retrieve my backpack and find Jake watching me. Our gazes lock. There's worry on his face. Despite his admission of technical ignorance, somehow I suspect he's made the connection. The same thoughts and fears are going through his head, too.

Chapter Seventeen

Micah repacks his bag and heads for the closest EM tower. "I'll ping everyone once I get in," he says. "And I'll send your Links the app so you can track each other, too."

"I don't want to track us," Jake says, still protesting. "And I don't want anyone to track me!"

"Think about it like this, Jake: This way, we'll be able to see any implanted zoms too. Not saying there are any here, but wouldn't you want to know if there were?"

"Lot of good it does us." He points at the lone zombie and says, "You still can't track the them. IUs don't have implants."

Micah shrugs. "IUs are harmless." He shoots me a look and winces. "Well, maybe with one or two exceptions. We still don't know if that one was a rogue escaped from one of the work details back on Manhattan, right?"

Jake frowns, obviously not convinced. "How about some company then?" he asks. "Besides, you'll be safer with someone watching your back."

Or watching over his shoulder.

"No, but thanks, Jake. You'll just distract me. Don't worry. I'll be fine. Go have some fun. You'd just be bored if you came with me." He checks his Link. "Let's plan on meeting back here around . . . two. If not sooner. Ping if anything comes up. We should leave by two thirty so we don't have to fight the current again."

Ash and Reggie are standing off to one side whispering to each other. I'm about to ask what they're planning on doing when she giggles and slaps his arm. Reggie glances over at us and grins.

"Ash and I are going to check some things out," he says. He looks around and his gaze stops in the direction of an old Holiday Inn. "Over there."

"Want some company?" Jake asks, again.

I roll my eyes. *He really is that clueless!* Then again, could Ash and Reg really be that horny? We've got a couple hours to explore the abandoned city and they're going off to mess around. *Really?*

Reggie shakes his head. "Naw, brah." He wraps his arm around Ash's shoulders. She looks so small standing next to him. "I think I can handle this alone."

Ash cocks her head up at him and smirks. "A bit overconfident, are we?"

Jake realizes too late what they're talking about. He turns to me and Kelly, his face red.

"No," Kelly snaps, before he can say anything.

"Why not? I said I was sorry about the zombie thing back there."

Actually, he didn't. But while I may be willing to let that slide, Kelly clearly isn't. "I don't remember hearing any kind of apology from you," he spits. "And even if I did— "

"Kel." I frown and tell him to cut the guy some slack.

He sighs and says, "Fine, you can tag along with us. Like a little puppy. It's not like I wanted to spend a little *alone* time with my girlfriend or anything."

"Really?" I say. "That's what you want to do?" I jut my chin out at Reggie's and Ash's receding figures. "Is that all I am to you is a sex toy?"

"That's not what I meant! I got something else in mind." He pats his pack. "But don't ask, because as I said, it's a surprise."

"Ooh, I can't wait."

He rolls his eyes.

There's a cluster of high rises due south of us a couple blocks away. Kelly points in that direction and says he wants to see how high up off the ground we can get. "Maybe we can see over the wall from one of the windows. Wouldn't it be cool to get a pic of Manhattan from here?"

"Pictures? That wasn't the type of surprise I was expecting," I say, but he just smiles like he already knows that.

Jake looks doubtful. "Shouldn't someone stay here and make sure our stuff is safe?" he asks.

"Safe from what? Look around you. Do you see anything that's going to mess with our equipment? Pigeons?"

"Zombies?"

We all turn and look at the solitary figure in the distance. It still hasn't moved.

"Are there two?" Jake says, squinting.

"Shut up."

"No, seriously." He lifts the binoculars and looks through them. "There are two of them."

"Let me see," Kelly says.

He looks for a moment, then shrugs. "There's two. But maybe the other one was standing behind the first and moved a little. At that pace, they'd reach us in, oh, about six weeks."

Despite what happened in the tunnel, I have to laugh. Besides, Jake's concern is misplaced. What would a couple of zombies want with a bunch of diving equipment? The only thing that drives them — drives their 'life force' or whatever you want to call it — is human flesh.

"It'll be fine," I say.

"On second thought," Jake says, "you guys go on. I think I'll just hang out around here."

"Yes!" Kelly says.

"Kelly, no."

He frowns at me.

"Safety in numbers. Remember? Jake should come with us."

"He *wants* to stay here."

"I don't think it's such a good idea, Kel."

"You didn't say that when Micah left, alone."

"Micah can take care of himself."

"And Jake can't? He's a big boy." Kelly smirks at him. "He seems to think so, anyway."

This makes my anger flare again. "Why are you acting this way, Kelly? It's Jake, not Reg! Or Micah." I whirl around to face him. "I don't know what's going on between you and Jake, but you both better knock it off!"

"I didn't do anything," Kelly complains.

"No, but if it weren't for Jake, you wouldn't even be here. You're being a thankless prick."

"Prick? I didn't even want to come here in the first place!"

"Hey, guys," Jake says, "I'll be fine. Really. You don't need to argu— "

"We're not arguing!" Kelly shouts.

"Stop shouting," I say. "You want the zombies to hear us?"

He laughs and makes a show of waving his arms and shouting. "Hey! Hey! Look! Brains! Come get some."

"Quiet!"

"Like your shrieking earlier wouldn't have drawn their attention?"

"Shrieking? You make it sound like it was over nothing."

"Guys! I— "

"You shut up! You weren't even there when I was attacked," I scream.

"You know something?" Kelly says, throwing his hands up in the air. "Fuck this. I can't take it. Stay here with Jake the Flake for all I care. I'm outta here!"

"Kelly— "

He stomps off.

I know I should run after him, but I also know that's what he wants me to do. This is all about him and Jake. It's about their false idea that I'm supposed to make some imaginary choice between them. I don't know why he's become so moody over the past couple of weeks, but it's really getting on my nerves.

"Fine!" I scream at his back. "Fuck you, too! And I *will* stay with Jake!"

I'm sorry as soon as it comes out, but then he turns back around and gives me this look. There's a darkness in his eyes that I can't ever remember seeing in them before. And sadness.

I expect him to yell back at me. I expect him react in kind.

But all he does is shake his head.

"I'm sorry," I want to say. I open my mouth, but nothing comes out.

"I'll be back in an hour," he says. "Or two."

Then he turns around and walks away.

Chapter Eighteen

"So who's G-ma Junie?" Jake asks.

"What?"

"I heard Ashley mention her to you earlier."

I flick a pebble from the railing into the water. It makes a soft plunk and sinks away. The sun's baking my back and my shoulders are starting to burn. Now that I've dried off I'm starting to sweat. I consider taking off the wetsuit completely, but I just can't be bothered.

"Ashley's grandmother," I tell him. "Was, anyway. She . . . died. This past spring."

He nods. "I didn't know."

I turn my head to stare at him, wondering why he'd assume he would. All he was to Ashley before this was her lab partner. It wasn't like they were friends or anything. And after this little jaunt of ours, it's likely she'll drop him like shoddy programming. I just don't see him continuing to be a part of our group.

On the other hand, I'm beginning to wonder if any of us will be able to go back to the way we were before all this. Kelly and I are drifting away from each other, faster and faster it seems. Meanwhile, Reg and Ash are looking more and more like a full-time couple, squeezing the rest of us out of their lives.

Even if we continue to hold it together, I just can't see how Jake might fit into the new scheme of things.

"What happened to her?" he asks. "Do you know? Where'd she get sent?"

I hear her voice again inside my head, telling me how she'd rather be a Player than be stuck on guard duty or sewer cleanup.

Probably the last words she ever spoke to me were that very wish.

I take in a deep, shuddering breath and peer out over the water. Except for the sound of the wind and birds, the whole place is quiet. Disturbingly so.

It's so hard to believe that in just a short dozen or so years, this entire island has gone from being overrun with thousands of the Infected Undead, killing the living, turning them into thousands more, to being this deserted. But it has. It's now just a pathetic, empty wasteland. Well, almost empty.

It makes me wonder why nobody has come to take the island back.

Actually, somebody did, didn't they? Arc Properties came, the big conglomerate of companies spanning every major industry there is. ArcTech. ArcWare. ArcBio. But what they wanted wasn't to bring the living back to this place. It was to fill it with more of the Undead: new zombies, stronger and fresher and faster, *implanted* zombies that can be controlled. Players.

What people are willing to do in the name of profit.

The Gameland arcade, at least according to Micah, is thirty miles east of us, centered on a place called Jayne's Hill. That's where the transmission tower is, the island's highpoint. But how he could know all that when the exact details are a secret is beyond me. Regardless, we're miles outside its boundaries.

I clear my throat. It's dry, so I take a drink from my collapsible water bottle before answering Jake's question.

"Her parents think she got sent to some remote place up in North Dakota. That's where they're guessing, anyway. I hear they use a lot of CUs there for border patrol."

"CUs?"

"Conscripted Undead. Or Controlled Undead. Depends on who you ask. Zombies with implants."

He nods. "When I go, I think I'd rather be one of the Omegamen."

I look him over for a second. "Yeah, well, die young and easy — a bullet to the heart or from massive internal injuries from an accident or something — and you can pretty much count on it. Or commit murder. That's the fastest way to become an Omega. You'd make a good soldier."

He smiles and straightens himself a little bit. "You think so?"

I roll my eyes.

"It's everyone's obligation to serve," he lectures me. "Just think how it would be if we had to send the living into battle."

I don't say anything. I know the arguments by heart. All too well, in fact. It doesn't help being related to the person who first proposed that the government militarize the zombies they'd created. Grandpa considered himself a hero for envisioning an end to all wars. But in the end, it broke the country apart and lead to its total isolation from the rest of the world.

"You don't get a choice," I tell him.

"They should at least tell you where they send your deceased relatives for their conscription."

"You know how the government is about sharing that sort of information. People would just want to go see them or . . . ." I let the thought drift off.

Or try to put them down.

"Unless you're highly connected, you can just forget about finding out. And if you're that connected, you can probably afford to buy out your LSC and be incinerated right away."

Jake turns around and leans his back on the railing. He makes like he's stretching, but out of the corner of my eye I can see him looking around. He stares off in the direction of the zombies for a moment.

"I suppose it could be worse," he says, lifting the binoculars to his eyes. "The idea of getting blown to bits somewhere in China or Texas gives me the creeps." He shudders. "At least if you're a sewer cleaner or a guard there's something to incinerate after your three years are up."

"Yeah, turkey jerky," I say. He gives me a strange look and I add, "You said it yourself: that's what happens to a zombie after standing out in the hot sun for a few years."

"The Undead don't know heat or pain."

"Maybe not."

"One of them's gone."

He hands over the binoculars and I look. "Probably crawled back into its hole. The other one hasn't moved at all."

We stay there like that for several minutes. The next time he speaks his words both surprise me and explain a lot: "I totally had a crush on you last year."

I turn to him, trying to keep my face neutral. Trying not to look surprised. I don't know if I succeed. "Look, Jake," I say. "You're a nice guy, but . . . ."

He waits. I want to tell him he's not my type, but it's such a cliché. And, besides, why would he tell me this now? Kelly and I had a little fight is all. It's not like we broke up, leaving an opening for Jake to step into.

I sigh and shake my head. "You wouldn't like me as much if you knew me better. I can be a total bitch sometimes."

"I don't think you— "

"How about we talk about something else for a while?"

He swallows, but the way he holds my gaze makes me feel like I'm the villain.

"You ever know anyone who got sent to *The Game*?" he asks after several more minutes pass.

And so we've come all the way back to G-ma Junie again.

I hand him back the binoculars and say, "They don't usually last very long." I know it totally doesn't answer the question. "A few weeks at most."

"I've seen Players on *Survivalist* leave *The Game* after only one day. God, that's got to be so embarrassing."

I can see why people would want to become Players. At least then a portion of the winnings goes back to the family. The longer you stay in, the more money you get. That's why Operators — gamers who control CUs — are willing to pay top-dollar for the best, the freshest, and the strongest zombies. Even if they have to obtain them illegally.

"Do you think it's true?" Jake asks, as if he can see inside my thoughts. "Do some people sell themselves into *The Game*?"

I shake my head. But once more it makes me think about G-ma Junie. I know it's just my own suspicious nature, but it was like she was there one day, a young fifty-three-year-old woman with a good eleven years left before her LSC, and then, the next day she was gone. Just . . . gone. And what's more, Ashley's parents suddenly seemed to have some extra money. How else could she have ever afforded a Ronnie Marx bathing suit?

But, no. I can't believe something like that. I just can't see G-ma Junie as a Player. No Operator would ever buy someone as old and worn out as she was.

I shake my head. "No, I don't think so," I finally reply.

Chapter Nineteen

Two more zombies have joined the first. We watch them, fascinated by their incredibly slow, patient waltz. We wonder what they're doing and why they seem to congregate in that one spot. What's there? Did an animal die there or something? Do they even eat wild animal meat if they can't get human flesh?

"It's like they're having a meeting or something."

"Yeah, discussing the weather. 'Hey, Bill, how ya feeling today?' 'Same as always, Frank. A little stiff.' "

Jake snorts.

"They must draw each other by their movement and sound."

"I guess we're too far away for them to notice us then."

I nod and squint at their tiny figures. They seem to appear out of nowhere, then disappear again, as if melting into the ground. But it's just an illusion, a trick of the distance and the shimmering air burning off the concrete.

Another half hour passes and the group has grown to a half dozen. We decide to call them a herd, although I actually prefer flock.

I try to tell them apart, but I can't; they're all burned a rich dark brown and are little more than skeletons.

Then we get the first ping from Micah:

<< IN! TRYNG 2 FND CUS. SNDNG APP >>

Jake and I install the program on our Links and open it. A map of the surrounding area pops up on our screens.

"How come I'm only tracking me?" Jake asks. He tilts his screen so I can see.

I look over, then down at my own screen. There's only a single red blip, and when I tap it, my name's the only one to appear. "Me, too."

I'm in the middle of sending Micah a note when my Link pings. Micah's already realized the problem:

<< SML GLTCH. WRKNG ON IT. PTNCE >>

"Glitch, right. In other words, 'Don't bother me. I already know.' "

Jake nods. "One of the others must've noticed it, and said something to him."

"Too bad. I'd really like to see where they are."

He clears his throat. "I'm sure he's fine. Kelly, I mean."

I know who he means. Yeah, I'm worried about my boyfriend, but I'm also worried about the others. I don't reply to Jake's attempt at reassurance, though. There's no way he could know if they're safe or not. In fact, his words only make me worry more.

"I should've gone with him."

Jake picks up his pack and says, "Come on. Let's get out of the sun." He glances nervously at the zombies, even though they're too far away to see with any clarity. "I'm broiling out here, and I'm not even wearing my wetsuit."

He heads for the closest building in the opposite direction, an old fossil fueling station. Perched over the collapsing structure is a big plastic sign on a long pole. Its bottom corner is shattered. The plastic is bleached and faded, leaving only the hint of the red and yellow logo. The remaining letters spell out HELL.

We duck under the canopy built out over the fueling stands, but the shade provides little relief from the heat. The air feels just as stuffy and dry and stale. There's not even a hint of a breeze. Jake kicks aside some trash to get to the door.

I'm surprised that all the glass in the windows and doors is still intact, but then I remember how quickly the infection overran the island, and how quickly the military came in and evacuated it. There'd be no one left to loot and ransack, nothing but zombies, and the IUs wouldn't bother with glass unless they were trying to get through it to someone still alive.

The irony doesn't escape me that the living can be so much more barbaric than the Undead.

Jake pulls a rusted metal trashcan loose from a tangle of wires and other debris. It scrapes along the cement. Underneath is a nest of spiders and mice, which scamper in all directions after being so rudely evicted. We take a few minutes to stomp the bugs dead.

"It's a tumble weed," he exclaims, holding one up by a branch. He tosses it out onto the cement apron, but it just falls, settling onto its bottom.

"I think you need wind for it to actually tumble."

He smiles, then yanks on the door. "Locked. So much for—"

The glass explodes and Jake jumps back, yelping.

I kick the remaining shards loose and duck underneath the push bar inside.

"You could've warned me, you know!" he yells at my back.

"Sorry. Now we're even."

"For what?"

"For playing dirty in the dojang. For not saying anything about the zombie back in Manhattan. For being such an asshole to my boyfriend."

Anger flares on his face for a moment. But then something flickers over it and the tension drains away. He grumbles a few words under his breath and follows me in.

It's dusty and dark inside, a dull twilight that even the bright sunlight outside can't seem to break. The shelves are still fully stocked, but there's nothing worth taking. Everything's at least a dozen years past its expiration date or brittle or mouse-eaten. Even the liquor looks questionable — not that I'd want it, even if I were a drinker. Just the thought of consuming anything that's been sitting in zombieland for twelve years makes my stomach want to revolt.

We wander up and down the aisles, stopping to check out the old magazines. Yet another relic of the past. Everything's digital now. Gone are the days of printed material, forced by the demise of the old postal system.

The covers of the magazines on top are nearly completely faded away, just the ghosts of images barely visible. I slide one out from behind the others. The colors are still vivid, having been protected from the air and the light.

"Here you go." I toss it to Jake, who deftly snatches it out of the air.

"*Playboy!*" He drops it like it's contaminated.

I reach down and pick it up. "You know how much you could get for this back home?"

Soft porn magazines like this were banned nearly a decade ago. There are Streams where you can find pornographic images, but it's dangerous to do so. Getting caught labels you a sexual predator and can add years to your LSC. A lot of magazines like this one, as well as others that had absolutely nothing to do with porn, like *Scientific American* and *Popular Science*, were blamed for the moral corruption of our society, which in turn was blamed for causing the zombie outbreaks. Puritan logic.

"They're illegal," he says.

"Yeah duh. Since when did you become such a prude?"

He shrugs. "They catch you with one of these . . . ."

"Yeah, yeah. They take another year or two or ten away from you. What does it matter anymore? They always find ways to add years. I don't remember you being so worried about it when we came here. What do you think they'd do if they caught us? Do you think they'd just chuckle and say, 'Nice try. Don't do it again, kiddies.'?"

He sighs, then picks the magazine up off the floor. "Real paper," he mutters, rubbing it between his fingers. "Snow."

The cover shows a tall, buxom, waif of a woman with skin as white as a two-week old zombie. Her lips are the brightest red I've ever seen. She's standing in a simulated pine forest, strategically placed snow-laden boughs covering her private parts. Barely.

I reach over and flip it open to the centerfold and read. "Miss March: Tatiana Lovinescu. God, what a name. Sounds like Titty Loving. 'This all-natural Romanian beauty boasts a bounteous— ' "

Jake pulls the magazine away. He gives me an embarrassed smirk before shoving it into his pack.

"You really are a prude, aren't you. I'll bet you're still a virgin."

His face goes crimson, but he doesn't answer. Instead, he turns and heads for the exit. "It's too hot in here."

I chuckle as I follow him out. Just as we reach the door, there's a thump from somewhere deep inside the store. We both stop.

He turns. Did you hea— "

"Shh!"

I lift my Link and thumb the screen to wake it. The app Micah sent comes to life, but it still only shows my little red blip and nothing else. Jake does the same with his, but gets the same result. Micah better get the tracker working soon or else it won't matter.

"What do you think it was?" he whispers.

I wait a moment, then swivel on my toes and head back to check out the noise.

"*Hey!*"

I gesture for him to be quiet.

The store is arranged in four separate aisles running front to back. I make a full circuit of the inside, taking an indirect route to the back, but nothing seems amiss, not until I reach the end of the furthest aisle and see a bunch of cans lying on the floor. Cans that weren't there before.

I try to blink away my panic. My blood is roaring through my head, sounding like a freight train. A zombie could be moaning right behind me and I wouldn't be able to hear it.

I look up into the mirror in the corner of the ceiling. From where I'm standing I can see nearly all the aisles. I slowly creep forward until I reach the fallen cans. Nothing moves.

I pick one up. The label slips off and whirls to the floor. It's all faded and half eaten away by mice and bugs. It's got to be stew or beans or dog food. Rust discolors it and it smells of mouse urine.

Reggie's voice speaks in my head. "Of course it smells like urine here," he'd once joked, after Kelly complained once too often to Micah about the sorry state of the basement bathroom in his house. "That's because you're in here. Get it? *You're in* here?"

Several more cans litter the top shelf, their labels similarly peeled or eaten away. Boxes of some other foodstuff sit nearby, holes chewed into their corners. Cream of wheat. They're completely empty. When I touch one, the shelf rocks and two more cans roll to the floor.

"Jessie?"

"I'm fine," I shout, straightening up. "It's cool. Just some cans that fell off a loose shelf back here. Probably mice." I toss the can I'm holding onto the floor and head toward the front door again.

The entire episode has set me on edge, though. I walk back, keeping my body rigid and my eyes trained straight ahead of me, even though I want to turn around and look behind. Even though it feels like I'm being watched. I don't want to appear frightened; I'm not sure which of the two Jakes will appear if I do, the overconfident one or his scared helpless twin.

The few steps it takes to reach him feel like miles, and my scalp tingles and my blood pounds and I'm sure I'd jump out of my skin if just one more can of dog food happened to fall off the shelf. Thankfully, it doesn't.

When we get back outside, I breathe a sigh of relief. He checks the time. "They should be back soon."

"What's your rush?" I ask, but I'm eager to see Kelly again, despite the way we'd left each other.

Jake reaches down and sweeps the broken glass off the step and sits down. "Might as well stay here in the shade before heading back over."

I pull out my Link. "I'm just going to ping the guys and see what they're up to. You should check on those zoms."

But he doesn't. He sits there watching me. From where he's sitting, looking up, I know he's got an unobstructed view. I'm wearing nothing else on top but my bikini top.

Despite his confession earlier — or maybe because of it — I pretend not to notice. Let him stare. It's nice being noticed for once.

Don't be like that.

It should be Kelly sitting there, not Jake.

It's not his fault.

My Link pings at me as I'm thinking these things, startling me. I jump and almost drop it.

"It's Kel," I say, and relief and guilt both wash over me at the same time.

"He coming back?"

"Yeah."

"What are you going to do when he does?"

"What do you mean?"

He fiddles with his own Link. "It's just past one. We don't have to leave for another hour and a half or so."

I type in a reply as I consider the question.

"I don't know. I hadn't really thought about it. I guess I was so wrapped up in seeing if we could actually come here that I never thought about what we'd do once we did."

But then I do think of something.

"Maybe we could find an old bookstore. You know how long it's been since I held a real book in my hands?"

"Books?" He shakes his head. "More contraband."

I finish my text and send it:

<< HURRY BCK. MISS U. SORRY >>

My Link pings almost immediately. It's Kelly again. I open the file, expecting a text message, but instead it's a photo. Seeing it, I nearly burst into tears. It's a picture of the surprise he was talking about.

I turn my back on Jake so he can't see me crying.

Jake gasps.

I turn just as he stumbles to his feet. His face is ash white.

"What's the mat— "

He grabs my arm and spins me.

My face grows numb and I drop my Link in shock. Not thirty feet away are at least a dozen Infected Undead. They lurch forward, heading straight for us.

And the spookiest thing about it is that they're making almost no noise at all.

Chapter Twenty

"Back inside!" Jake hisses.

"Are you crazy? We'll be trapped! We need to run for it!"

Their numbers have already doubled, as more of them stagger around the corners of the building, closing the gaps.

I grab Jake's arm and twist him back around, but he resists. He dives through the broken glass door in a panic, kicking my Link out of reach as he does.

I watch it skitter to the feet of the closest zombies. They don't even bother with it. Their feet grind it into the pavement. But Links are manufactured to withstand pretty much everything short of a nuclear bomb, so I know it won't break. Still, Kelly's photo is on there. I take a step toward it before Jake grabs the sleeve of my wetsuit dangling down.

"Jessie!" he screams.

"No, let go!" But by the time I've recovered we've lost any chance to escape through them. Now they're three deep and pulling in tighter. I might be able to burst through them, but I can't risk getting scratched or bitten. I let Jake pull me inside.

He runs to the nearest aisle and wrenches the metal shelf from its bracket. Items crash to the floor. He carries the shelf over and slips it between the door's push bar and the frame.

"That's not going to hold them!" I scream, but he ignores me and goes for another.

The first zombies are banging on the corners of the display windows, edging their way closer. The glass thuds, making dull, hollow noises. Those in front get pushed down by those behind. Their hands whisper over the glass, sounding rubbery and dry. A single moan rises from them, triggering all the others. The sound quickly grows.

One of them stumbles against the glass. Its skin is so shriveled and brown that it looks like bark. It opens its mouth and its teeth and tongue are as black as licorice. Its head hits the ground and pops like a puffball beneath the feet of the approaching horde.

"We're trapped!" I shriek. "We need to find another way out. Jake, listen to me!"

By now he's wedged three of the shelves into the opening. He pushes a fourth sideways, locking them all into place.

The zombies fill every spare inch of the window and have reached the door. They rattle it. The metal creaks and groans. They slap feebly on the glass, but there are so many that the glass vibrates. It bulges inward, then back out, as if it's breathing. More zombies push against the ones in front and the glass bulges in again, crackling.

I slide behind the counter and tear through the dusty trash and mouse droppings underneath. There in the darkness I find exactly what I was hoping for: a pistol.

I yank it free. Its cold edges are rimed with flakes of reddish powder, gritty beneath my fingers. A shiver runs through me. But it's not blood, it's rust. Dust and cobwebs fill the muzzle. A quick check of the chamber tells me it's loaded. I don't have time to inspect the magazine. I pray it's full and that the rounds inside it are still good.

When I was nine, my grandfather took me to the shooting range, defying my brother's vehement wishes that he wouldn't. But Eric was only seventeen then, a self-proclaimed pacifist, and Grandpa was a lot more imposing of a figure than he's become since then.

"Your brother may be a spineless idiot, Jessie," he told me then, "but I know you're not. You need to learn how to fire a weapon. You need to know how to defend yourself."

Call it whatever you want — irony or spite, or maybe even resignation — but right after Eric graduated from high school, he went and enlisted in the Marines. He volunteered to fight in Mexico and got sent with the Omegamen to China. Now he wears a gun on his hip. Granted, it's an EM gun, but still. He's not the young man I remember growing up knowing. He's . . . changed.

But Grandpa still calls him spineless.

"Did Mom say it's okay?" I'd asked him, hoping against hope that he wouldn't answer. Or if he did, that he'd lie. I was breathless with excitement at the idea of firing a real gun, but I knew it was my duty as a daughter to ask for my mother's permission. Of course, I could never remember a time when she'd ever actually taken that role seriously, but I still felt an obligation to give her the right to refuse something like this.

I'm not so naïve anymore.

Grandpa must've seen the look on my face because he said, "It's okay, young lady. Your mom's fine with it. I already asked her." I didn't challenge him. We were both complicit in a crime that was not of our own doing.

It wasn't until many years later that he'd tell me it was the same gun my father had fired the night he died. I don't know that it would've made any difference to me then. I doubt it.

I wrench open a drawer and look for the box of the remaining rounds inside. There has to be one. You can't just buy a few bullets.

"Jessie!" Jake yells.

The moaning and banging from the front of the store has grown even louder, more insistent, spurred on by the racket Jake made before and continues to make now.

I take a quick look toward the front. The metal shelves are just thin sheets of aluminum and already they're beginning to buckle against the weight of the zombies pressing against the door.

Jake flies past me and disappears past one of the displays near the back. I hear a door slam open, then the telltale sounds of bathroom stall doors being flung wide. Somewhere in the back of my mind I'm thinking what a crazy-ass time it is to be taking a dump.

"What the hell are you doing?" I scream, still searching for the rounds.

"There's a window in here!" Then, "Shit! They're outside in back, too. We're surrounded!"

"Get out here, Jake!" I scream, alternately searching and checking the windows. The only thing that's saved us from being overwhelmed is the zombies' weakness. They're slow and desiccated, weakened by years of not feeding. Their movements are stiff and jerky. Or at least they were. They seem to be waking up.

It's the noise! Stop making so much noise!

I need to find that box of spare rounds.

"There's a back door here," Jake shouts. "Christ, where the hell are they all coming from?"

Draw them to the front!

How?

I spy the cash register. The bullets are probably in the back of the drawer.

I try to open it, but without electricity, the thing's locked tight and won't budge.

There's a fire extinguisher sign in a back corner. As I hurry over to it, I hear the first splinter of glass from the front, a sharp report, followed by snapping sounds. I fling my head back. It's just a crack, but the windows won't hold for much longer.

I pray that my hunch is right.

"Jake, get the fuck out here! I need you!"

I find the extinguisher, but the object I really want is hanging on the wall next to it: an axe. I yank it free from the mount and sprint back to the front.

I don't even slow down. I raise the axe over my head as I run and bring it down on the register. It crashes into the counter, missing the target by half a foot. I curse just as the window explodes inward. Glass rains down on the horde as the Undead tumble inside, slicing several of the zombies. But it doesn't stop them. It doesn't even slow them down.

The first ones trip and fall. The ones behind begin to climb over them, but they're pushed down by the third wave. The growing mound of Undead acts as its own speed bump, buying me precious seconds.

I wrench the axe free from the countertop and bring it up again before slamming it down on the register. The ancient machine chimes and caves in, but the drawer stays closed. Two more quick swings and it finally pops free. But now the first zombies are less than ten feet away. I raise the pistol, cock it and squeeze the trigger with one hand while the other yanks the drawer fully open.

Coins and bills shower to my feet. The gun goes off, rocking me onto my heels.

My hand is shaking so badly that the shot goes wide. A hole opens up in the chest of a zombie further back. The bullet passes easily through it and shatters the unbroken window, unleashing another torrent of the walkers into the store. The zombie I hit rocks backward and falls. It's quickly overrun by others.

"What the hell was that?" Jake screams from the back.

I aim and the second shot finds the forehead of the closest zombie. Its head explodes in a powder. The skull shatters and the thing collapses. I get off two more shots and drop two more of them before I see Jake out of the corner of my eye, skidding up the aisle.

"This way!" he screams, pinwheeling his arms.

I manage to fire another three rounds, but only one zombie goes down. The noise is making them go berserk. Their moans are shrieks of desperation and their movements are much more focused.

"You can't shoot them all!"

I know he's right. There's no way I'd even be able to reload the clip, even if I had a thousand rounds. They'd be on top of me in a second. And my shoulder already burns from the recoil.

How I wish I had an EM gun.

I duck quickly down and sweep my hand over the floor until it encounters an object with some heft to it. I lift it and shove it into the elastic waist of the wetsuit without looking. Then I grab the axe in my other hand and run toward Jake, knocking a withered zombie in a faded too-large muumuu out of my way. She tips and falls in slow motion.

"I'm coming," I shout, and I pray Jake's not just planning on barricading us in the bathroom.

He's standing beside a metal door, one hand up to stop me, his eyes glued to the tiny opening.

"Jake, you better have a plan, because they're fucking coming!"

He reaches down and grabs something off the floor. It's a tire iron. The other hand holds a—

"Is that a toilet plunger?"

"Yeah." He kicks the door open.

I don't have time to say anything else before we're rushing out into the bright sunlight.

There are only a handful of zombies in back now, the rest drawn to the front by the gunshots. They turn as one as we skid out onto the loose gravel behind the store and begin their advance. They're moving frightfully fast, faster than the ones we first saw in front.

I step around Jake and with a quick shot from the pistol dispatch an Infected wearing the still-recognizable remains of a tattered business suit. Like the others inside, its head explodes in a fine powder, not the spray of gore I keep expecting. A strange powder that lingers in the air before slowly drifting back to the ground.

"What the— ?" Jake exclaims. "Jesus, that's sick!"

"Jesus is dead and he ain't coming back! Now move!"

Another zombie quickly takes the place of Business Suit. I swing the axe one-handed like a sword, not caring if I hit the thing with the flat side or the edge of the blade. Instead, the spike sinks into the monster's face. It falls, pulling me down with it.

Jake reaches over and grabs me, keeping me from falling right onto the blade, but knocking me in the head with the plunger. He swings his other hand at another zombie. It spins around.

He swings again, and the plunger strikes it on the shoulder with a dull *thwop*, accomplishing absolutely nothing. The zombie reaches out. Jake thrusts straight at its face. I expect to see the plunger stick, but the zombie tumbles over backward instead.

"Really?" I shout. "You couldn't find anything better? A toilet brush, maybe?"

"Closest thing to a *dahn bohng* I could find," he says, referring to the short sticks some fighters use in hapkido.

"I prefer the long staff."

"You're doing just fine with that pistol!"

I stumble back to my feet. He points to an opening and we sprint for it.

His backpack bounces up and down and from side to side, making him look awkward. He twirls his plunger and tire iron like batons.

The zombies that were heading around the sides of the store have changed direction and are now staggering toward us. Jake heads for the widest space between them, then suddenly veers off in a new direction.

"Where are you going? Our gear is the other way!"

"Yeah," he puffs. "Exactly." And I realize he's right. We need to lead them away, not toward it. Otherwise we'll never be able to leave.

The Holiday Inn rises up before us. I wonder if Reggie and Ash are still inside. They should've finished by now and come back already. Do they even realize what's going on out here? How could they have not heard the gunshots?

And then I envision them in a hotel room, unaware that it's filling with zombies, the sounds of their lovemaking attracting them from other parts of the hotel.

"Where'd they come from?" I pant. "Jake? Jake, stop! We can't just keep running around like this. We need a plan. And it has to include the others."

He slows, nodding, but doesn't stop. I jog to keep up with him.

"We might be running directly into even more of them."

He puts on the brakes and I plow into him.

"Jesus, Jake!"

"I don't know where they're coming from, Jessie." But there's something in his eyes, an accusing look. He thinks this is my fault.

"They heard the glass breaking."

"It's not your fault, Jess."

He takes a moment to assess our situation, turning in a full circle. Other than the zombies swarming the refueling station, the place still seems empty, but now we know we can't trust this perception.

The zombies we can see number at least fifty by now. They've turned and are heading toward us, as if we're magnets.

There are so many of them. So many, and they showed up so suddenly. Where were they hiding? And why? Were they just trying to stay out of the sun? Were they . . . planning?

I can't believe I'm even entertaining such thoughts. The Undead don't think.

"Jake?"

He's staring at the Holiday Inn. "That's where Ashley and Reggie went, isn't it?"

"Yeah, and that's why we can't go there. We'll lead the zombies right to them."

"What if they're—" He stumbles backward, swearing and shaking his head as some variation of the thought I'd had moments before comes to him. "I hope they didn't come from inside there."

"You need to ping them," I say. I feel naked without my Link, vulnerable. Helpless. "We need to warn the others."

He glances back at the zombies, his eyes still crazed with fright. "Shit," he repeats, but he nods and pulls out his Link. As he does, he starts walking, cutting off to the right and toward more open ground. "Keep an eye out for me, Jess," he says, gesturing with his free hand. He babbles almost incoherently into the Link.

"They're getting closer, Jake. We need to move."

"Okay," he says, slipping the Link back into his pocket.

We start jogging again.

"You told everyone?"

"I tried Micah. No time to key in anyone else."

"You spoke to him? Is he coming?"

"He wouldn't accept. I left a message."

"Damn it!"

I notice we're heading for the tower, the same one Micah said he was going to earlier. It's at least a quarter mile off, far enough away that we'll easily lose the zombies before we arrive.

I'm not sure this is the best plan, however. I don't like having my back up against the wall — literally — and we don't know if there are more zoms in front of us. On the other hand, we need to lead them away, anywhere, just not toward the gear.

And we need to do it quickly, because it now looks like there are close to a hundred of them.

Chapter Twenty One

Jake's Link pings just as we reach the first row of taller buildings. They look like warehouses. We slip around the corner of one and find the street deserted. It's a row of shops. Wouldn't it be ironic if one of them was a bookstore?

We stop to read the message:

<< ON MY WY >>

Jake quickly tries to open a voice line, but Micah doesn't answer.

"Come on, man!" he grunts, pacing anxiously. "Why won't he accept? Damn it!"

He's practically screaming with fright. I try to calm him down. The last thing we want to do is to draw out even more zombies from wherever they might be hiding. "Just leave a message. We need to keep moving."

"Stay there, Micah," he tells the recorder. "We're coming to you."

"Stay there?" I say. "No! He needs to come back. We need to get back to the equipment and leave!"

Jake pockets his Link. "Not with those things just standing there!"

He brushes past me to peek around the corner. "Damn it. They've stopped. Stupid things. They're just shuffling around in random directions now."

I look for myself. From the relative safety of our hiding spot, I can rest a moment and get a better look at them. Their clothes are faded and hang on them in rags. If they have any at all. I notice how weathered they are, dry and dark and timeworn, barely much more than skeletons. The plastination of their flesh from the infection is obvious. The Infected Undead, victims of the outbreak thirteen years ago, the ones the military left behind. Chocolate, sexless, men and women and children. Chocolate monsters.

I put my hand on his shoulder. "Jake—"

"We've got to draw them away from the tunnel," he says, shaking my hand off. Before I realize what he's doing he's back out in the middle of the street, waving his arms and shouting. "Hey, you! Over here! We're over here!"

"Jake!" I whisper, darting out and grabbing his tee shirt. "What the hell are you doing? Stop it!" I check behind us to make sure the street is still empty.

He ignores me and shouts even louder. He jumps and waves and screams. The urban canyon we're in begins to fill with moaning sounds. They echo all around us, amplified by the closeness of the buildings.

Stiff as wooden dolls, the zombies turn and make their way toward us.

From a distance, they all seem agonizingly slow. But now I can see that this is wrong. Not all of them are slow. Some move faster. But that's not the only difference. They have a waxier sheen to their skin and their muscles don't seem as atrophied. They have the same aimless shuffle as the rest, but their steps are longer. Their legs swing just a fraction of a second brisker. Their movements are more precise, more... focused. Fresh zombies? But how?

I don't know, but these are the ones we need to worry about.

"Let's circle around," Jake says. He grabs my arm and turns me. "Maybe we can find a dead-end alley with a fire escape or something."

"You want to use us as bait to draw them into an alley?"

"You'd rather stand and fight?"

I shake my head. "I'd rather just go home."

"Better if we herd them into an alley than leave them scattered about."

"Only one problem," I say. "They're not cows. And they're already too scattered."

"I never said it would be easy." He points to a pair of tall buildings with a narrow space between them. We hurry over, but as soon as we turn the corner we can see that it won't work. The other end is open.

"We're wasting time, Jake," I say. "We need to find the others and get out of here."

We stumble back onto the main street. The first of the zombies are already there, a half dozen lurching toward us, their movements deceptively quick.

"Fuck," Jake pants. "Does it seem like they're getting faster?" He backs away.

"Just run," I say, but he's right. They are fast, and getting faster.

We both turn into the alley and run. When we reach the other end, we turn again, angling perpendicular to the tower and the tunnel as best we can. Our footsteps slap against the road, echoing off the buildings, sounding like clapping.

"This way!" I hiss, reaching out for Jake's arm and turning to the right. His shirt slips from my fingers and he continues straight down the broad road. "Jake!"

He spins around. His eyes are wild, but he follows me. This constant swinging of his between lucidity and panic is driving me crazy.

"We need to get back," I gasp. "We can't worry about Micah. He'll catch up to us."

He looks at the gun still in my hand. "How many bullets do you have left?"

"I don't know." Then I remember the box and pull it from my wetsuit.

"Paperclips?"

"Shit!" I throw the box away. It breaks open and bullets spill out, scattering across the pavement. "Damn."

Jake hurries over and starts to pick them up.

"No time!" I yell. "Leave them. Even if we can just grab the gear and get it into the water, that's better than waiting. It's our only chance!"

New footsteps echo around us, someone running. We both look up in time to see Micah sprinting past us on the street ahead. He doesn't see us.

"Micah!"

But he's already disappeared.

"Shit. *Micah!*"

Micah's head reappears around the corner. He looks up the road in the direction he just came from and makes a snap decision. He sprints toward us. "Get out of here!" he screams. "Go back!"

The moaning is growing louder. The street behind us suddenly fills with walkers. "Run," Micah shouts.

Jake and I spin around. The zombies crowd into the street, lurching madly at us, moaning and shrieking and clacking their rotting teeth.

"Shit! Aw, shit!"

"Calm down, Jake," I tell him. "You need to calm down."

"We're trapped!"

Yeah, whose fault is that? But I don't say it. I push him toward one of the buildings.

Lifting my arm, I bring the axe down on the display window of a bridal shop. The gowns inside are yellowed and dusty. When the glass shatters and falls on them, they tear easily and flake to the floor.

"What the hell is it with you and breaking glass?" Jake screams.

"Just get inside!"

Micah reaches us. He doesn't hesitate. He vaults over the high brick sill of the display window and into the store. Glass crunches under his feet. He stops, turns, and reaches down to help us in.

Jake hesitates.

"Get your goddamn ass in here," Micah growls at him as he pulls me up.

I don't stop to help. I head for the back of the store, looking for the emergency exit or loading door or whatever the hell they've got. It's our only chance to evade the zombie horde.

I hear footsteps behind me.

"I cut myself on the glass," Jake wails, holding his arm. Blood seeps through his fingers. It looks like a nasty gash, but I can't worry about that right now. "Why'd you pick this shop? The one next door had a bigger window."

I don't have time to explain it to him. I kick down a door marked "Employees Only" and find what I'm looking for. There's an emergency exit across the room, but I see that it's secured with a chain and a padlock.

I swing the axe behind me.

"Give her some room, dummy!" Micah shouts, pulling Jake back. The axe barely misses Jake's head as I bring it forward in a sidearm chop.

The blade pings off the chain. I try again, but the chain still holds.

Micah grabs my arm. "Give it to me. From the front of the store, the sounds of moaning and breaking glass come to us.

Jake goes over and tries to barricade the inner door.

Micah lifts the axe with both hands and brings it down on the latch that holds the chain to the jamb. It bends. He tries again, taking smaller, more precise swings. Finally it shatters and falls away. He hands the axe back, then reaches over and pushes the door open.

The alley is narrow. It's also open on both ends, but it's empty and there aren't any zombies in sight. We edge out of the shop. We could very well be trapped, but at the moment it's our only option.

Micah lifts a board from the ground and wedges it against what's left of the doorknob, locking the zombies inside. Then he pulls out his Link.

"What the hell are you doing?" Jake shrieks. "Calling for a pizza?"

"Just keep an eye out!"

I do a quick scan. There are no windows in this alley, no way to easily break into another building if we find ourselves trapped. And the fire escapes are well out of reach above our heads.

"This way," Micah whispers. He puts his Link in his pocket and leads us toward the street he was running down earlier. "We'll probably have to take a few out," he says. He glances at the gun in my hand. "But there shouldn't be as many as you had chasing you. What the hell did you do? Wake the entire island up?"

I give him a look of such frustration that he quickly turns away and starts running up the road.

He's light on his feet, almost as quiet as a cat. For someone who spends ninety percent of his free time in his basement getting drunk and hacking games, he's surprisingly athletic.

We reach the end of the alley and peek around the corner. A few zombies are milling about. Apparently these are the "slow" ones.

"Felt like a hundred of them before," he says. "Nowhere as near as many as were chasing you." He smiles. "Must be that perfume you're wearing." He pauses, then adds, "Jake."

"I'm not— "

I interrupt his protest. "Where the hell *were* they? That's what I want to know. And what woke them all up? Was it noise?"

Micah shakes his head. "Couldn't be. I didn't make any. But when I stepped out of the tower I was totally surrounded. Damn things were all over the place, like they knew I was there. Scared me so badly I just ran right through them. That's when you pinged me, Jake."

"Did you get scratched or bitten?"

He shakes his head.

"Shouldn't we be moving," Jake hisses, "instead of just standing here making small talk?"

Micah takes another look around the corner. "Wait another minute and see if the rest of them clear out."

He pulls his Link out again, reminding me that I'm still missing mine. I just hope there's a chance to go back to the fueling station so I can get it.

"The others should be there by now," Jake says. "Did you let them know what's happening? Is that what you're doing?"

Micah shakes his Link and frowns. He taps the screen. The frown turns into a scowl. "Has anyone pinged either of you?"

I shake my head and quickly tell him about losing my Link. Jake checks his, then shakes his head, too. "Nothing."

Micah looks up in the sky, as if the answer to whatever is bothering him is written there. "I can't reach them. I hope they're okay."

I swallow my panic. "The road's almost clear," I tell them. "Wait just a couple more—"

But then a horrible grating noise comes from behind us in the alleyway. The board Micah had wedged into place snaps and flies off, spinning into the air and hitting the opposite wall. The door swings open, vomiting zombies into the road.

"Go!"

Chapter Twenty Two

"They're there!" Jake shouts. "I see them!"

He's outpaced us and is now sprinting along a good hundred feet ahead of me and Micah. I want to tell him not to get too far ahead, but I'm too out of breath. Even Micah's beginning to gasp. But Jake's still running like he could go on like this all day.

"There's Ash and Reg!"

Alarm bells ring inside my head. *Where's Kelly?*

"They've already got their suits on."

Now I'm glad I left mine on.

Micah and I top a small rise and now I can see the others. They haven't noticed us yet. But just as I'm about to warn Jake not to shout, he calls out.

Kelly appears from around the back of the car. The trunk's open and he's already fully geared up, even though we hadn't planned on leaving yet. Then I see the bodies of a dozen zombies scattered about them and can guess what happened.

"Jessie!" He starts running toward us.

I wave him back. "Get the gear!" I yell, but my voice sounds too small. My throat is dry. Out of the corner of my eye, I see movement. The slower zombies that had been tracking us earlier are now emerging from between the buildings where we first entered the row of shops. Directly behind us are the faster ones.

"Get the gear!" Micah echoes, though a lot louder.

The three at the car turn and gather the rest of the equipment. Jake is the first to reach them and he quickly grabs his wetsuit. Micah and I reach them moments later.

Jake's struggling to get his legs in. Reggie screams to let him help. Ashley runs over to Micah with his suit while Kelly comes to me with my mask.

"Hurry up, Jessie!" Kelly shrieks. I want to slap him. What does he think I'm doing?

I'd started pulling my arms into the suit even before I got there. They slip easily on.

Jake's yanking at the second leg, screaming in frustration. His suit doesn't want to go on. I realize it's because his suit is still wet but he's not. He hasn't even broken a sweat. "Get some water!" I scream at Reggie. "Wet down his skin."

The closest zombies are about a hundred feet away now.

I zip my suit up, then shift the gun from my other hand. I aim at the closest zombie and squeeze the trigger. The gun clicks.

"Shit! Where's my mask?" I toss the gun away, but keep the axe.

Kelly hands me my mask, along with his goggles. I push them away. "They're not going to fit me!"

Reggie scrambles back up from the water's edge. He hurries over to Jake with his hands cupped, but the water spills out before he gets him. The two of them start fighting over how to get the suit on Jake. Reggie just starts shoving parts of Jake's body into places inside the wetsuit where they don't belong. Jake's shaking with terror now, useless. Even from where I'm standing I can see that his suit is twisted. He'll never get it zipped up. Reggie tries anyway. He gives the zipper a massive tug and it rips.

"Never mind," I scream. "Get into the water!"

Kelly has taken my axe and run over to the first zombies. He takes two out and is working on a third. They seem to appear out of nowhere, swarming, their moans filling my ears.

"Kelly!"

He throws the axe at another and sprints back, snatching our backpacks from the ground and hurling them out and over the water. "Let's go!" he yells, as they splash down.

Ashley and Micah are already climbing down the fence. Ash reaches the water first and plunges in, pushing her gear and flippers ahead of her. I snatch my flippers and head for Jake and Reggie, who are still stupidly struggling with the suit.

"No time! Into the goddamn water!"

I grab two more pairs of flippers as Kelly gets their packs. Everything gets hurled over the railing. Reggie kicks at a zombie while pushing at Jake, who's practically sobbing by now and babbling. The zombie gets back up and comes at them again, but it has to push past several of its comrades.

Reggie swings the spare equipment bag at them, bowling them all down.

I grab Jake and yank him away just as another zombie reaches for him. Its blackened fingers close over empty space. Its momentum trips it, but it doesn't stop coming.

"Wrong way!" Jake screams.

"You're going over!"

I grunt and push him over the railing. He flips in mid-air, then splashes into the water.

A hand rakes my back. Instinctively, I step away, even as I reach back, grab, and pull. I use the attacker's own weight against itself. But I realize only too late what I've done as the zombie follows Jake over the railing. I try to pull it back, shouting, "Lookout!" But its arm rips from its socket with a dry popping sound.

There's a splash. Ashley screams. Or maybe it's Jake.

The next zombie lurches at me, but then Kelly launches himself at it and it flies off to one side.

"Go!" he shouts.

"Not without you!"

"I'm coming."

And we vault the railing.

The surface comes up fast. It's a roiling, chaotic mass of water and air as Jake kicks himself away from the zombie. Micah is slashing at it with his knife. Reggie is swimming over, but without flippers he's moving too slowly. Our gear bags slowly gather against the wall of the overpass, pushed there by the breeze and the waves that everyone's thrashing is making.

"I'll help Jake," Kelly yells. "Get your flippers."

I swim over and find them. I've just managed to get the second one on when there's a splash right beside me. I look up and see a zombie tilting over the railing right over me.

"Jessie!"

I kick away from the wall just as it falls, narrowly missing me. Then it seems to be raining zombies as more and more of them tumble over the railing in their attempt to reach us. Some sink immediately, while others bob near the surface. They thrash. Their moans turn to gurgles as their throats fill with water.

"The gear!"

"Forget the gear," Reggie says. He's got his flippers on now and is swimming Jake's over to him. "We need to go! Now! Look!"

Dozens of the Infected Undead now line the overpass. The line presses forward. A dozen bodies fall and another line takes its place.

"Shit!" Ash screams. "Oh, my fucking god where are they all coming from!"

Jake has finally managed to get the rest of his gear on and has gathered with the others about thirty feet from the overpass. I'm still off to one side, separated from them by twenty or so feet of water and several floating zombies leering at us.

"We need those spare canisters," Reggie roars, holding up his mask, but he doesn't move to get them. Nobody does. To do so would be suicide, since our bags are floating against the overpass. There's no way any of us can reach them. "These still have the used ones!"

"You didn't switch out the canisters?" Jake screams. "What the hell were you doing?"

"Never mind that," Kelly says. "Which bag are they in?"

"We can't!" Micah shouts. He turns to Jake. "You said these last about three hours, right? Well it took us half that to get here. I hope for our sake you're right."

He then shouts over at me to stay put. "We'll meet underwater." Then he instructs Kelly to swim over to me. A minute later, Kelly surfaces a few feet to my right. He grabs my hand.

Micah checks his Link one last time and curses. "Where'd the time go?"

"I don't care," Ashley says. "I'm going now!"
We all nod in agreement. It's now or never.
"But this time," Kelly shouts, "we all stay together."

Chapter Twenty Three

We meet underwater and join hands. The scene around us is surreal: A panoramic movie of zombies drifting down into the darkness below. They lurch and twist at us, looking like dying earthworms dropped into a child's bucket. They remind me of autumn, of rotting leaves sinking into a lake.

Then I remember the old video stream Reggie found one day while searching through some archived footage from the first part of the century: people falling from a burning building, plummeting to the ground, dropping, dropping, until the whole building collapses into a ball of dust that reaches to the clouds and turns the sun red.

"Is this real?" I'd asked, horrified at the images. "This can't be real."

Ashley asked her G-ma Junie about it and G-ma Junie told her to hush and never bring it up again. "Destroy the video. It's illegal to speak of things that happened before."

We slip between the falling bodies. It's easy to evade them. They can't swim. They only drift down, and then they slip along the bottom as the current catches them.

I remember the one that attacked me on our way in. It had acted differently. It seemed like it knew how to swim. But maybe that's just how I'm remembering it.

Is it still alive? Is it lying on the bottom of the tunnel somewhere, unable to move because of its severed spine? How long could it stay there like that? Forever? Would the fish eat it?

The pile of zombies directly beneath the overpass is so large that they continue to rain down. The seething mass writhes and splashes, bodies disengaging themselves as the zombies struggle against one other. We don't stick around to watch. We swim quickly past them and they ogle back at us, looking almost resentful, their mouths gaping and their tongues lolling out. Their eyes black with death, full of longing and hunger.

Earthworms, I tell myself. *That's all they are.*

Except earthworms don't want to eat you. At least not while you're still alive.

The current gently pushes us forward. Already it's very weak, suggesting it'll turn soon. We'll end up fighting it again the closer we get to Manhattan.

We enter the same tunnel we came through earlier. Between the six of us, only two flashlights remain. Reggie holds one as he leads the group into the darkness. The rest of us form a chain, each holding the hand of the person in front: Reggie, Ashley, me, Kelly, Jake, and finally Micah in back. He holds the other flashlight. We push ourselves to the limit, kicking hard with our flippers to get away from that terrifying place.

I'm thirsty and tired, faint from hunger. My feet hurt and my knees burn from all the running we've done. My arms ache from swinging the axe. I can't see very much, and what I can see is blurry.

But I don't want to see. I keep my eyes closed and concentrate on kicking and for once I'm glad that Reggie is the one leading us out. He's always been the physically strongest among us.

We arrive near the place where the zombie attacked me. I only know this by instinct. Or maybe I imagine Kelly's grip tightening on my hand. I keep my eyes closed. It makes the time pass quicker. Soon. Soon we'll be home. I never want to come back.

I concentrate on my breathing — in and out and in again — timing my kicks to keep the rhythm going. The beat becomes a part of me, a part of my own living rhythm, until I no longer have to think about it.

Images gradually creep back into my mind, so slowly and stealthily that I don't realize it at first. The zombies in the store, the way their heads exploded like sacks of flour, like they were so old that they'd completely dried up inside. How could they still be . . . alive?

The ones that attacked us after we'd returned to where our gear was hadn't been like that. The faster ones. One of the zombies Kelly had beheaded had made a wet squelching sound when it fell. A thick, deep red fluid had oozed from its neck. It was a fresh zombie.

I shudder.

Reggie stops a couple times, both times asking us via Link if we're all okay. Kelly notices that I don't have mine and gives me a curious look. I shrug and hold out my empty hands. He types something into his screen, then shows it to me:

<< LOST? >>

I nod. He shakes his head. I'll need to figure out how to explain it to the Department of Citizen Registration when we get back. The questionnaire for a lost Link is over a thousand questions long.

The second time Reggie stops, I notice the drag on us. The current has stopped pushing at us. And while it isn't yet pulling us back yet, the lack of assistance combined with our fatigue is slowing our progress. We've depleted our energy reserves.

I'm especially beginning to feel it, since I didn't eat earlier. My legs cramp. There's a stitch in my side. Any adrenaline I'd been running on has long since evaporated away.

Micah gives Reggie an impatient look and gestures at him to keep going. We quickly reform our chain and carry on. We don't know how much longer our cartridges will last. Once more, I close my eyes and let the others guide me.

The minutes pass. Then I feel Ash and Kelly release my hands. I open my eyes, thinking we've reached the end. But everything's still dark, except for the two beams of light, spreading out.

I push myself toward the source of the closest one. Jake's face emerges from the gloom. I grab his hand and hold on. He stops and looks at me, confused, tension filling his face.

He holds up his Link and types:

<< BLOCKED >>

He reads my frown immediately, since I have no goggles to distort my eyes. Gripping my hand once more, he points downward with the light. Below us is the faint outline of the rear of the old bus we'd passed on our way in.

I look up again. The debris dam looms over us, tall and massive. It stretches all the way to the ceiling and spans the tunnel from one side to the other. A large tree trunk pokes through it, its stunted roots looking like a gorgon's head, a nest of unidentifiable flotsam trapped within its tentacles.

Jake swings the light over to the side. I'm barely able to make out Kelly and Reggie. They're at the opening we used earlier, but now it's blocked. I can see them trying to move something. Ash and Micah hover nearby with the other flashlight. Reggie must have given Jake his light to locate another opening.

I urge his hand to point the beam over the surface of the logjam once more, looking for another way through. Below us, a stream of mud eddies out of a narrow gap beneath the bus. In just the few seconds we hover there, the cloud spreads up to meet us.

A new alarm rises up inside of me: the current has shifted.

Jake realizes this too. He yanks the light away and swings it back up at Reggie and Kelly. They've got a corner of what looks like a box spring mattress and are pulling at it, trying to pry it loose. Jake makes an urgent noise with his throat, but we're too far away for them to hear it. I begin to kick my way up toward them.

I reach Ash just as I start hearing a soft plinking noise below us. I look down and see Jake urgently banging the handle of his knife on the flashlight, trying to alert the others. Ashley hears it and turns, inadvertently shifting the light in Micah's hands away from Kelly and Reg.

Just then there's a low grinding noise, massive and ominous. I feel it in my bones, and I sense, rather than see or hear, the pile beginning to shift, the low grinding of several tons of material moving against itself, pushed forward by the strengthening current, unrelieved now that its only opening has been obstructed.

Jake makes that urgent sound in his throat again, but Kel and Reg don't hear. He swims past us and stabs them with his light. They keep working on pulling the mattress free.

Now I see the first fingers of muddy water beginning to surge past them. I grab Ashley's arm and pull her away.

Her eyes narrow at me in confusion. She pulls back.

A loud metallic moaning sound comes from the bottom of the pile. The bus lurches. Ash makes a sound in her throat. I gesture that the boys need to hurry.

Jake reaches Kelly and pushes him away. They begin to wrestle with each other. Reggie turns and stares as if they're crazy. His body stiffens. He watches them do their slow motion fight for a moment before he tries to separate them.

Something shoots through the small opening. It wraps around Jake's head. He tears it away and tries to see what it is, but it slips from his hand and disappears into the gloom. Kelly takes the opportunity to move away.

I wave my arms, but they don't see me. Jake grabs Reggie and points down, but Reggie can't see what he's pointing at; it's too dark. Behind them, the mattress bulges out. Jake points again and waves his hands in a sweeping motion. Reggie shakes his head. Jake gives up and tries Kelly again.

Behind them, the mattress twists. Suddenly, it shoots out of the gap, hitting Reggie in the back. A bubble of air escapes his mouth and his mask sinks away. For a moment he looks unconscious, but then his head whips around and his hands go to his throat.

I dive downward into the darkness, not knowing where I'm going, only moving by instinct. I sweep my arms around until I feel something light brush against the back of my hand and I stab at it until my fingers wrap around the tube connecting the cartridge to Reggie's mask. It seems like a miracle, but I'll take it. I turn and kick my way up.

Reggie is still struggling. He's drifting away toward the darkness, but nobody else sees him. Kel and Micah are moving to the opening. They see that it's clear again. Jake swims up to them, still gesturing.

A series of thumps comes to us from all around. They echo dully and ponderously, sounding like they're coming from the other side of the heap. A loud scrape follows. Everyone stops what they're doing to look around. Everyone but me and Reggie.

I swim desperately toward the gloom, towards Reggie's fading ghostly shape. I get one last glimpse of his eyes just before he disappears: they're wild and bulging behind his goggles.

I hear the sudden release of air and I know Reggie's using the air in his goggles. There's another release. Then a third. How many more before it's empty?

I need to find him.

Kelly's suddenly there, pulling me back toward the opening. He spins me around. I see Micah hanging onto the edge of the metal cage, kicking against the current, casting his light inside to see if it's clear all the way through. The mud swirls through in thick clouds. But the current looks too strong. Even if it's wide enough for us to swim through, how can we?

I push Kelly away and turn. I kick into the darkness.

Then the light turns toward us. I see Reggie up ahead, his hands clasped over his mouth, his cheeks bulging. His eyes lock on me, and the mask in my hand. He kicks weakly, but he's still drifting further away.

I finally reach him. He clutches me desperately. Even starving of air, his grip is like steel. I thrust his mask into his face. He takes it and exhales explosively into the canister, then inhales. The canister wheezes from the force of his breathing. I fear he'll burst the bag inside.

In he breathes. Out. Repeating the cycle as I try to tow him back toward the heap. But it's against the current. It's like towing a boulder through quicksand.

Reggie recovers enough to help me. Finally we reach the opening. Items are falling all around, tumbling down around us or being swept up in the rush of water through the gap.

Kelly's got his Link out. He flashes the screen at us:

<< 2 DANGERUS >>

He points back the way we came.

Ashley shakes her head. She grabs for Kelly's arm and misses, tries again, grabs his ankle. I can see her shaking her head vehemently at him and pointing in the other direction. There's no way she's going back to Long Island.

I feel Reggie push against me. He's still shaking, but stronger than he was even just a moment before. His recovery is amazingly quick. He grabs the edge of the metal cage and pulls himself into the opening.

The urgency is clear in Kelly's eyes, but Ashley takes the opportunity to jockey her way into the gap. The current pushes her back and she somersaults. But then a hand shoots through the opening and grabs her, turning her around. The gap shifts; the cage begins to crumple.

Micah grabs me and shoves me toward the opening. Then Kelly follows me. I pass Reggie inside, wedged in a tiny recess. He helps us through. Just in front of me, I see Ashley's flippers disappearing out the other side.

Something flutters past my face. Then something else drags across my arm, scratching me. I kick and strain and grab onto anything that'll keep me from sliding back. I'm acting on adrenaline. We all are. There's nothing else left.

I push and pull and kick. Then I shoot through the opening and find calmer water. Ash returns with a pole. She pokes it through. Kelly grabs it and pulls himself out.

There's a loud rumble and everything shifts several feet. Ashley loses her air and lets go of the pole. I take her place while she recovers.

Just as the entire debris pile shudders, Micah emerges. There's a loud crack and a rumble and the cage collapses upon itself. Micah's flashlight gets ripped from his hand. It tumbles away, then winks out. Complete darkness descends over us.

Someone grabs me. A Link screen glows, showing me Kelly's face. He pulls me clear of the pile.

Jake! my mind screams. He never made it through.

Kelly points. I catch a glimpse of Ash holding her Link before her, the mask now back in her mouth: she's trying to put her goggles on. Micah's helping her.

I don't see Reggie or Jake.

Then Reggie appears in the faint glow of Ash's Link. We join them, clustering close together.

<< JK? >>

We all shake our heads.

Reggie types:

<< CANT STAY. CANSTER FAILNG >>

Kelly shakes his head. He points at the pile and begins to swim toward it. But then he stops and turns. He pushes his mouthpiece deeper in and sucks. Panic rises in his eyes.

I can also feel it. I don't know if it's just because Reggie mentioned the canisters failing or if it's actually happening, but I'm suddenly feeling light-headed, just like I did on the way over. There's a dull pressure behind my eyes and I fight the urge to breath deeper and faster. How many more breaths do I have left?

I snatch Ash's Link and quickly scroll through it to find Jake's contact. Pictures of people flash by, some I recognize, others I don't. One goes by so fast that it doesn't register at first, someone I know. Someone Ash shouldn't.

Then there's Jake's image. I ping him.

There's no response.

Micah grabs Ash's hand and pulls her, but I won't let him. I try Jake's Link a second time.

Still no response.

Now we have no choice. We'll all die if we stay. Even if we leave now, we might not make it.

Then Ash's Link lights up.

<< DON'T LV ME >>

Micah shakes his head. There's no way through the dam. Jake's on the other side, but he can't reach us. And we can't reach him.

Ash crumbles, but Reggie grabs her arm, shakes her, points frantically. *We need to go!*

We form a chain again. I take one last look back, hoping for something, some sign that Jake has found a way through. I think I see a flash of light. I stare for a moment, but there's nothing but darkness.

We swim on in total darkness. I can't know if I'm crying because my tears just melt into the filthy, salty water. And yet I do know. I'm crying because we've left Jake behind.

And yet I swim on.

One by one, our cartridges fail. We share the rest between us until all we have left is the one unused one that Micah still had on his belt. And still we haven't reached the opening.

We each have to be wondering, with the five of us using it, will it last?

Reggie guides us with his hand on the wall of the tunnel. We pass the one mask between us: front to back to front again.

And then, just as it begins to fail, the darkness in the tunnel lightens just a tiny bit. I'm half delirious by then, starved of oxygen, exhausted, grieving. We all are. But it's not the light of the tunnel opening we see, it's the light from Ash's Link receiving one final message:

<< IV GONE BAK >>

We each see it, but we don't stop to think about it. Survival is paramount — *our* survival. It's the one thought we all share and can't argue about.

But now a second thought settles in, a doubt, waiting for the first moment when it can capture our full attention: How can we just leave Jake behind? How could we live knowing we did?

We can't.

We have to go back.

ACKNOWLEDGEMENTS

As always, my *undying* thanks to all of the devoted staff of Brinestone Press for their keen eye and gentle but firm touch in helping me bring these stories to life, for believing every step of the way that I could speak with and for the dead.

To my devoted fans and followers on Twitter, especially the zombie apocalypse junkies. Everything's better with the #zombie hashtag.

http://twitter.com/saultanpepper

And to my faithful friends and fans on Facebook.

http://facebook.com/saul.tanpepper

‡ ‡

My deepest gratitude goes to my family for their unflagging support, especially my beautiful children.

‡ ‡ ‡

ABOUT THE AUTHOR

‡

Saul Tanpepper is a writer of speculative fiction for teens and adults. A former molecular geneticist originally from Upstate New York, he now calls Northern California home.

If you enjoyed GAMELAND: *Deep Into the Game*, please check out his other works, available in digital and paperback formats.

For more information about the author and his writings, please check out his website:
http://www.tanpepperwrites.com.

‡ ‡ ‡

CURRENT TITLES IN THE GAMELAND SERIES

In this prequel to S.W. Tanpepper's GAMELAND series, a molecular geneticist creates an experimental antidote against the virus for reanimating the dead.

But to test it he must first infect himself.

⭐⭐⭐⭐⭐

[A] very technical story that would do justice to anything written by Michael Crichton.
—D. Dalton

Golgotha is available as a digital ebook at Amazon.com, Barnes & Noble, Sony, Kobo, and Apple iBookstore.

Also available in digital & print formats from Amazon.com in the collection *Shorting the Undead & Other Horrors*

Six hackers break into GAMELAND, a virtual reality survival gaming arcade in Long Island's zombie wasteland. But while breaking into *The Game* is easy, breaking out turns into a hell of a killer.

⭐⭐⭐⭐⭐

There are lots of twists and turns and the writing is outstandingly good.
—Rabid Readers Reviews

8-episode package available as a digital ebook at Amazon.com, Barnes & Noble, Sony, Kobo, and Apple iBookstore.

Available in print format from Amazon.com
December 2012

To find my books on-line, scan the image below with your smart phone, or type in the link provided

Amazon

US
http://amzn.to/OTU1Fx

UK
http://amzn.to/R5CXfo

DE
http://amzn.to/OiEYdf

Barnes and Noble
http://bit.ly/RtzMEK

Kobo
http://bit.ly/TNIWZX

Apple

US
http://bit.ly/Rqsssp

UK
http://bit.ly/UBeTVS

CA
http://bit.ly/RYF44S

DE
http://bit.ly/OxdVXa

AU
http://bit.ly/TCGiql

Smashwords
http://bit.ly/P4SEWi

Sony
http://bit.ly/P6eNI8

Diesel
http://bit.ly/Q6JOEl

Made in the USA
San Bernardino, CA
23 November 2018